MONKEY IN THE MIDDLE

An Amos Walker Novel

Loren D. Estleman

A Tom Doherty Associates Book
New York

monkey in the middle

Copyright © 2022 by Loren D. Estleman

A Forge Book
Published by Tom Doherty Associates
120 Broadway
New York, NY 10271

www.tor-forge.com

Forge® is a registered trademark of Macmillan Publishing Group, LLC.

The Library of Congress Cataloging-in-Publication Data is available upon request.

ISBN 978-1-250-82717-3 (hardcover)
ISBN 978-1-250-82718-0 (ebook)

Our books may be purchased in bulk for promotional, educational, or business use. Please contact your local bookseller or the Macmillan Corporate and Premium Sales Department at 1-800-221-7945, extension 5442, or by email at MacmillanSpecialMarkets@macmillan.com.

First Edition: 2022

Printed in the United States of America

0 9 8 7 6 5 4 3 2 1

To Betty Morgan
in loving memory

There are some secrets which do not permit themselves to be told.

—Edgar Allan Poe,
"The Man of the Crowd"

ONE

He was leaning against my car, ankles crossed, hands in his pockets, the universal body language of casual indifference. I ought to have been sore, and might have been except for the day I'd had; but it just seemed like too much effort.

I wouldn't have had time anyway. As soon as he spotted me he sprang up straight, igniting spots of color on his cheeks; he was afraid he'd scratched the chrome. That should have embarrassed me more than it did him. Road salt had been eating at it since before the century turned.

In the right mood I'd have raised a blush, just to be sociable; but the kid had enough to go around.

You can't fake that. If he could—wasn't just what he seemed—it might have saved a world of hurt down the line, and possibly a life or two. But there's no use dwelling on the past.

He was all corduroy and denim and scuffed Hush Puppies, eyeglasses with blue plastic rims; the Halloween store had run out of pirates and Darth Vaders and he was stuck with Teaching Assistant. His hair was chipmunk-orange and grew in every direction. Mom had given up trying to train it—and not too long ago, either. I had an unexpired passport older than he was.

"Mr. Walker?"

The voice was a surprise. Anyone who looked like him should come with a cracked tenor, not a light baritone. They'd gotten their voice chips mixed up back in the toy factory.

"You were perched on his car," I said. "What do you think?"

"I—your vehicle registration's on record with the Secretary of State's office. I went there after I saw your web site. I couldn't make up my mind whether to go up and see you. You settled the point just now. You *are* Amos Walker?"

By "up" he meant two flights of stairs to my office in the pile across the street from the weedy lot where I parked the Cutlass.

Web site. I'd forgotten I had one; I paid the monthly fee along with the rent and utilities every first Monday and never thought about it afterward. In a weak moment I'd agreed to let Barry Stackpole build it. I hadn't looked at it since the day it went up, and on the evidence neither had anyone else until now. This kid looked like job security—and that neighborhood looked like an English garden.

I said, "I'm closed. Come back some other time to some other place and pick on some other car."

That day I might as well have stayed home, where doing nothing and not getting paid for it is more fun. That's summer in Detroit. Everyone who can afford to leave town has fled, and those who can't take their business to the cops. Domestic beefs, carjackings, and party shootings don't leave much work for a private detective. The hours go by on a dragline.

Capped this time by the phone call I got just before quitting. News like that always comes when you're at low tide.

He rummaged in all the pockets he had, retrieving wads of limp currency until he had enough for a stack. Homebound traffic wheezed past, shimmering in the heat, while he arranged all the bills until the grim gray faces stared skyward.

He had me at Ben Franklin. I wouldn't have climbed back up all those stairs for anyone less than U.S. Grant.

His name was Shane—of course it was—and I gave him points for not sneering at the décor, the tasteful earth tones of dirty olive and oil spill. The hollows in the wooden seat on the customer's side of the desk were made for his narrow haunches. Three stories down, hip-hop and reactionary politics drifted out the open windows of cars with busted air conditioners and over the sill into the office. A lukewarm breeze from the window fan I'd bought to replace the old oscillator made his thistly hair stir east, west, north, and south. It was fascinating to watch.

He was almost as restless as his hair. His eyes kept returning to the door we'd just come through. It was an ordinary enough door.

"Shane Sothern," he said. "Maybe you know it."

"Sure. Of the Port Huron Sotherns. Your great-great-grandfather posed for the top of the Penobscot Building."

His smile shook me. I'm usually a better judge of character. That pile of tender on my blotter had changed all my plans for the evening. But I could get drunk anytime.

"My people were stock clerks and factory workers," he said. "I'm the first in my family to attend college." He reached inside his ribbed sportcoat, snapped open a newspaper clipping, and pushed it across the desk.

It was a feature from the front page of the entertainment section of the combined Sunday edition of the *News* and *Free Press*, the print smeared from handling. He shared a two-column color shot with a balding man whose fringe of white hair came to his collar, the two facing each other across a battleship-gray typewriter that looked as if it came with a pilot light. Sothern looked younger yet than today, but the man on the keyboard side was seventy years old in every photo I'd ever seen. He'd had a lock on all the best-selling book lists since whales had feet. The caption read: *Gerald Rickey consults with Shane Sothern on a point of local history.*

Sothern got up and came around the desk, leaning over my shoulder and mouthing what I was reading, as if he'd written it himself; never losing sight of the door. "It ran last December. That's why I thought you might know me."

"I was being presented at court. Collaborator?" I returned the clipping.

"Nothing so grand." He went back and perched on his chair like a pigeon on a ledge. "I approached him when he spoke at the library downtown, to ask for advice. My work kept coming back from magazines and book publishers along with the usual impersonal regrets. I was just a kid; it never occurred to me I might be putting him on the spot. I even brought a briefcase full of manuscripts on the off chance he'd read them and give me some tips. I'm still surprised he didn't have me thrown out of the place."

"He read them? Offered encouragement?"

Came back the blush. "He encouraged me to give up writing. He said I lacked the divine spark."

"What the hell's that?"

"He said if I had to ask, I didn't have it."

"Nice guy."

"Oh, but he is! And he was right. If he hadn't been honest with me, I'd still be struggling. And he said I had a gift for research. In one afternoon online or at the library, I could dig up more useful material than he could in a week; he said that. God knows how he knew, just from reading my stuff. He admitted it was a talent he lacked. So he hired me as his researcher, and right away his reviews got better. Critics who'd been dismissing him as a pander to the masses complimented him on his eye for atmosphere and detail."

"Isn't that just reading?"

The eyes behind the glasses got bright. They were blue then, the same shade as his frames; they'd looked colorless before. "Anyone can read. Jerry said I had a knack for bringing back not just what he told me to get, but piles of color that brought the facts and figures to life. Last year he sent me to look up a street in Kansas City, Missouri, find out when it was paved and with what, asphalt or macadam or cobblestones. Well, while I was doing that, I came across an account of the day Buffalo Bill brought his Wild West show there. Along the parade route he spotted a local youngster in the crowd and invited him to share his carriage. The boy was Walt Disney."

He paused, expecting me to show interest. I obliged.

"I told Jerry," he said, nodding approval: "You know, the greatest showman of the nineteenth century imparting advice to the greatest showman of the twentieth."

"That happened?"

"No one knows what they actually talked about. It *could* have; that's the stuff of historical fiction. The passage was only three lines long, but Jerry turned the idea into a novel. See, most researchers would've brought back just what was asked for and left the rest. Played fetch. What *I* did required imagination, which is the most important tool a writer of fiction has. All I needed, and didn't have, was the ability to put it into practice."

"What's the split?"

His face went flat as a plank. "Split?"

"The take. The dividends—royalties, I guess you call them. The good press must have boosted his sales. How far did he cut you in? I don't guess it was fifty-fifty."

"He pays me a straight salary."

I drew a pencil from the navy mug I'd swiped from police headquarters, scratched my ear with the eraser, stimulating my cortex. I was starting to get the drift.

"Sweet deal—for him. He shares the credit and cashes the checks. Respect is for the dead. Get a lawyer and cut a better bargain. He'll tell me what's evidence so I'll know it when I fall over it. I don't have your imagination."

His eyes got as big and blue as enamelware. "Oh, I don't want to *sue* him! He's not the only name author who farms out his prep, but he's one of the few to acknowledge it. I didn't ask to be in on the interview. He invited me. I'm happy with the arrangement. How much do you think publishers pay a fledgling writer? Nowhere near what he does."

"So what am I supposed to do to earn"—I thumbed through the bills—"this starter fee? Five hundred a day's my going rate."

He paled a little, but he said, "I'll have to manage it. There's no other choice. Mr. Walker, there are lives at stake."

The pencil was doing nothing for my brain. I blamed the pencil. I put it back in the cup and told him to start again.

"From the beginning?"

"Skip Disney. Give me the rest. All of it this time."

TWO

erald Rickey had nothing to do with it, as it turned out.

After dozens of years on the *New York Times* list, and twenty-odd Hollywood adaptations—including several remakes—the eighty-year-old novelist had announced his retirement. I had to ask his apprentice what a writer did when he stopped writing.

"I wondered the same thing," Sothern said. "When any other prominent figure leaves public life, it's usually to write his memoirs. He said that since he'd told most of his life story between the lines of his fiction, he was pumped out on that subject. He hates golf, doesn't fish, and gets sick on cruise ships. Since he grew up on a farm he has no interest in gardening. Just between us, I give him six months before he gets tired of all that me-time and goes back to the keyboard."

"Meanwhile you're out of a job."

"I don't have to be. As soon as he made the announcement, I was swamped with offers by other writers. Apparently, since that feature piece ran, the rumor is I'm some kind of good luck charm; as if talent and experience had nothing to do with Jerry's success. I never fail to be surprised by how little writers know about writing—when it comes to success, I mean. Even the old hands cling to the belief that there's some kind of mystical process involved. Oh, they grumble about tightwad advertising budgets, skimpy print runs, even sabotage in-house—editors jealous of their colleagues' track records, personal animosity, political agendas—but an astonishing number of professionals who should know better think there's some kind of genie in a bottle."

"That sounds like Rickey talking, and I don't even know him."

This time the rosy cheeks passed almost unnoticed. I had to remind myself not to hang the tag *predictable* on him. I'd already made that mistake once. "You're right. I'll have to come up with my own clichés if I'm to make anything of myself."

I got out a cigarette, just to play with; eight idle hours had smoke-cured my throat like kielbasa. I needed something to do to keep from booting him toward some kind of point. That seldom works. Most of the time you have to let them drift in search of a current.

He said, "I'm not desperate for money. Jerry presented me with a generous severance package, to hold me over until I decide what I want to do. Well, I have decided. I'm tired of doing the spade-work for others. I'm not a novelist; I've made my peace with that. Now I want to turn what I've learned about digging up facts toward a career in journalism."

"Gutsy move," I said. "Considering what's happened to news-papers."

"The Internet gets the blame for making them obsolete, but it's not just that—part of it's their own fault—and it's not just newspapers. I'm sure you're aware of what's become of reporting in our time. The media have given up any pretense of objectivity. Everyone's got an axe to grind—it's the same axe, really—and the hell with laying out the facts and letting the public come to its own conclusion. But the public isn't stupid; it knows what's been going on, which is why journalists rank right around career politicians when it comes to trust. That's the market I intend to tap with my book."

I'd heard all this before, from Barry Stackpole, although "the media" in plural and "the public" in singular was new; I supposed young Sothern had done his research on that. Barry would know. In the years since we'd served together in uniform, he'd written for the *News,* hosted his own TV show on cable, piloted a web site, and drawn a lot of attention to a podcast, expanding his specialty from organized crime to terrorism to domestic intelligence; not that he'd taken me into his confidence as to how they differed.

I tapped the cigarette on the back of my hand and lit it. Later I'd cauterize my scraped adenoids with Old Smuggler.

"What are you working on?" It was the polite thing to ask. Also it might swing the conversation toward some kind of shore.

He pursed his lips. He probably thought it made him look coy.

"I don't like to discuss work in progress. Jerry says it's like letting hot air out of a balloon, just when what you most need is lift. But this one has me concerned for myself."

"Concerned how?"

"It's kind of in the way of a—well, of a threat."

This was progress; but it was like snaking out a drain with a noodle. "Is it a threat or isn't it? If it is, talk to the police. They get paid to listen, and it won't take anything out of your savings."

"Oh, I know all about how the police work. I've spent more time in the precincts than a repeat offender. They don't call it the 'blotter' for fun. It soaks up everything they hear and stays out on the counter for anyone who wanders in to read. The bureaucrats had their own version of Facebook before anyone thought to invent the personal computer."

"That's the attitude that keeps me in cigarettes," I said. "The cops can tell Oprah to take a hike when it suits them, especially when there's a celebrity in the picture."

"Jerry's got nothing to do with why I'm here." He stared. "Are you trying to talk yourself out of a job?"

"No, just counting my thumbs and waiting to hear what the job is."

That got me nowhere, but I'd dealt with writers before. There's a better way to get them to open up.

"What's the book about?"

He did that thing with his lips again. He wasn't playing hard to get, just arranging his vocabulary. They're always doing that. It's a wonder more of them don't fall down open manholes.

"I prefer not to go into specifics, as I said. But the theme is that those of us born before nine-eleven have lived in two different Americas: The one where terrorist activity was something that happened on the other side of the world, and the one where it can happen to us anytime, anywhere in the U.S.

"That's a watershed, Mr. Walker. Even at the height of World War Two, with thousands dying overseas, Americans at home shopped, went to the movies, took walks, went for drives in the country—there was gas rationing, of course, but when they stayed home it was because of that, not fear of bombing. They refused to live in a bunker. Two great oceans separated them from the slaughter."

He paused just long enough to breathe. Having found his string finally, I wondered how I'd get it to stop.

"And that's how they—us!—behaved from colonial times right up until the twenty-first century; concerned, of course, for our neighbors far away, but largely unconscious of any threat to ourselves. Visitors from the Old World couldn't get over how we Yanks just went on about our business, secure as babies in our little womb; they thought we were naïve, but they envied us. Now we know different. We've given up all our conceits about privacy and individual liberty, accepted restrictions on our rights as citizens of a free nation in return for the illusion that our government was protecting us. *Americas in Collision,* that's my working title: two countries occupying the same geographical space, each bearing little resemblance to the other."

I'd listened, sitting back in my swivel, inhaling carcinogens and contributing to the golden stain on the ceiling. When the silence stretched far enough to indicate he'd finished, I screwed out the butt in my ashtray. "How old were you when the planes hit the World Trade Center?"

"Three; which is the age most experts agree is when we begin storing memories. My very first was of my parents crouched in front of the TV, watching the towers collapse. I was in my mother's lap, and she was squeezing me so hard I couldn't breathe. You could say my physical distress was symbolic of what everyone in the country was going through at the time."

"What I meant is that idea of yours is a chunk for someone your age to bite off."

The strategy was to put him on the defense. Nothing infuriates youth like drawing the age card. Everyone who comes into my office is a locked safe. Cracking it takes patience and study.

But Shane Sothern was Fort Knox in a Ziploc bag, or thought he was. He sat back, smiling. He'd gored the bull, slain Goliath, shelled the pistachio nut without even a gap in the seam to get his thumbnail into. He spread his hands. "That's my advantage. I'm just old enough to remember how much the earlier generation was shaken up by what happened that day, and just young enough to be able to bring a fresh viewpoint as to why. That's the line I mean to take when I offer my book to publishers."

It was getting dark, and the temperature had dropped. I leaned over to switch off the fan, then put on the lamp on the desk. The light reflected off the varnish, leaving dark hollows where his eyes belonged and giving me a glimpse of how he'd look at forty. It wasn't just a trick of the light. Whatever had brought him into my orbit had shaken him up as much as 9/11 had our two generations.

I had him then. I asked him who was following him.

THREE

You can't get a good reaction out of this generation. They don't shock, or at least pretend they don't; years of high-action films have taught them how to behave. Instead he slung another look back over his shoulder.

"It's a door," I said, "not a clock. It doesn't change. Who are you expecting to come through it?"

"I'm not sure. I guess that's why I'm here."

He stopped there, expecting—what? Concern? Sympathy? More omniscience on the part of a grizzled old gumshoe? That little heap of travel-worn scrip on the desk was looking more and more like rent for my patience.

"Not the guess I'm looking for. What is it: man, woman, bloodhound, a cable bill? Pay-Per-View can haunt you the rest of your life."

"I haven't actually seen anyone. It's just a feeling I can't shake."

I didn't sneer. A man who follows people for a living, and is often followed by them, can't claim sole title to that tingle at the base of the spine. "What else?"

"Someone broke into my apartment and searched it."

"Take anything?"

"Not that I could tell right away; maybe later, when I miss something I don't use all the time. Somehow I doubt it. It isn't something I could report to the police, even if I trusted them. I mean, whoever it was didn't dump out drawers or rip up upholstery or pull framed pictures apart. The place was in the same mess I left it, nothing specifically out of order, but I have a way of folding clothes and stacking them, and I had the distinct impression they weren't put back right. Well, can you picture the conversation if I made a complaint?"

"What kind of neighborhood do you live in?"

He got cagy again. "I don't see what that has to do with anything."

"Shane, I get paid by the day. If I spend most of this one giving you detective lessons, the PTA will file a complaint against me for teaching without a certificate. There are blocks in this town where the insurance premiums will cost you a kidney. If you live in one of them, move. That's advice I won't charge you for. Full-time bodyguards are another way to go, but they're expensive, and they didn't work for JFK."

"It's a respectable building in a middle-class neighborhood," he said. "There's a Neighborhood Watch and a regular police patrol. I can't remember the last time I heard someone was broken into."

"Good for you. What've you got that would interest a second-story man with something on his mind apart from loot? Writers make notes: records of interviews, hunches, plans for the week ahead. Any dynamite there?"

He smiled, that same pain-in-the-ass smirk, and patted his chest. He was a mugger's dream. "I keep all my notes on my phone, and it's always with me. Whoever went through my place did it when I was out." The smile twisted sideways and dropped through a crack.

I nodded at that. "You're scared he'll come back when you're *not* out. Back up your notes, put them in a bank safe-deposit box, delete all the dynamite from your phone, and give the phone to him if he comes back. If you're the kind that keeps his mouth shut—and you sure have with me—he doesn't know what you've got and what you haven't. You go your separate ways, you report the home invasion to the authorities, and you stick this small fortune here in front of me in the same bank with the box. This is a one-time-only deal I'm offering, on account of I'm in mourning. I just found out an old friend died and I'm not in the mood to haggle."

"I'm sorry about your friend, Mr. Walker. I have friends too. That's who I'm concerned about. Even if this person gets what he thinks he wants, he won't stop there. I'm not alone in this thing."

I sat back again, stretching a fresh cigarette between my hands. I didn't remember taking it out of the pack. "What is the thing? Give me nouns, names. If it's terrorism, identify the terror."

"I can't give details. Can't you just follow me for a while, see who's following me already, and go from there?"

"That's a conga line, not an investigation. What if you're casting more than one shadow and I get in between them? I don't spring back up as fast as I used to. I'm not Wile E. Coyote. Even when I was, I had a fair idea of what I was up against. Just because I put a price on my life doesn't make it cheaper than yours." I pushed the bills back across the desk.

He left them there for a moment, then gathered them in his fist and stood.

"I'm sorry I couldn't give you what you wanted. It's not mine to give. Going to the police would bring about everything I want to avoid. I won't deny I'm afraid for myself, but I'm just as afraid for—other people."

The door was three steps away. He used up most of a minute getting there. That was supposed to give me a chance to change my mind.

Someone had broken my cigarette in half. I dusted the loose tobacco off my palms into the tray. "Tell her good luck," I said.

He hesitated half a beat before letting himself out. I waited until

I heard his feet on the stairs, then got up and went to work earning the money I'd given back.

Adventure fiction to the contrary, confidential detective work falls more or less equally into two categories: sitting and walking. There's not a lot of romance in staking out some anonymous door, playing percussion on the steering wheel with your fingers, munching energy bars, and burning tobacco, if you're lucky enough to be a smoker. And there's not much more to be found in following someone who doesn't know he's being followed. You don't even have the drama of ducking into doorways when he happens to turn around, or faking interest in a window display; that doubles your chances of being spotted. Instead you just keep on walking and fighting the urge to whistle.

So far, Shane Sothern wasn't a student of *The Family Circus*'s Jeffy: He plotted a steady businesslike course west along Grand River, walking briskly under the streetlights but in no apparent hurry, and never once slowed to look back in the direction he'd come from. It was as easy and uneventful a tail job as I'd had in months.

Which put my back up. If he'd told the truth about being followed, he'd have turned top every few yards. It put my back up, but it didn't surprise me. From start to finish he hadn't come any nearer the truth than a convict who'd found Christ. I was only shadowing him because curiosity's the most important tool in my bag and it needs sharpening now and then. And I craved distraction.

The foot chase ended at Woodward, where a cross-town bus blasted to a stop just as he got to the curb and he climbed aboard. The timing might have been accidental, but I didn't think so; it would be the last load of the day. Only natives to the route know the schedule and measure their pace to avoid wasting time at the stop. The riddle had stumped more than one Nobel Laureate visiting from out of town.

I boarded just behind him, while he was shopping for a seat with his back turned my way, and shoved over a passenger near the front, getting an enraged grunt for the effort, but also a place to sit. No further complaint, though; putting up with a certain amount of rudeness is worth what you save on taxi fare. My seatmate, an ursine type in a knit cap and wool coat that made me break out in a sweat from proximity alone, crowded closer to his neighbor and dived back into hibernation in his three-inch portable screen.

It was the tail end of a long, sodden day that had begun at 5:00 A.M. at eighty-two degrees and humidity to match, with the city sweating through all its pores. The atmosphere hung with stale exhaust, cracked leather, and imperfect hygiene. You couldn't smoke aboard anymore, but the specter of Chesterfields, Dutch Masters, and Zig-Zag papers fed your addiction from deep in the upholstery. Someone had a flask; a gust of fermented grain cut through the stagnancy like the wind from behind compost, and was just as quickly gone. The driver's tired, pink-rimmed eyes searched the faces in his tilted mirror for the source, whether in disapproval or thirst wasn't clear.

It had been months since I'd used public transportation. I don't know what keeps it going, apart from the would-be johns who'd had their cars confiscated for soliciting prostitutes on the street. In Detroit, even the poor drive automobiles, leaving the People Mover—the late Mayor Young's electric train set—to tourists visiting Cobo Hall and the Fisher Building, and the buses to the elderly and weary, shuttling back and forth between corner markets, the casinos, and wherever they called home. In between were the blind pigs, numbers, girls, and maybe even a beer after the bars closed. Anytime, day or night, the city squirmed like nightcrawlers after a heavy rain.

The last time for me—and it struck me like a blow to the chest—
she'd been alive. It caught me looking. I had made my peace, or
thought so. I'd gotten the call ninety minutes ago and it had felt as
if she'd been dead a year. And here it was again, the wound burst
back open and gushing.

I turned then, coughing into my fist to cover the movement. It
was unprofessional. Shane would have to pass me to get off; there
was no need to risk tipping him that I was aboard. But I needed to
derail my train of thought.

Luck was with me. The kid who looked like he smelled of chalk
dust was staring out his window three rows from the back, watching the scenery deteriorate from theaters and municipal buildings
to public housing; the pipe dream of a dull-witted former governor who knew nothing of meth labs and crack houses, now waiting their turn at demolition; had been waiting for decades.

The bus stopped. I turned back just as he got up, and when he
walked past, steadying himself with a hand on the back of my
seat, I found interest in what my neighbor was looking at on his
phone. I got up before he could tell me to get my own and stepped
off as the driver reached for the handle that closed the door, into
the Third World of Northwest Detroit.

FOUR

I should've brought a flash. The streetlights there were spaced out like teeth in a jack-o'-lantern and a third of them hadn't cast anything but a shadow since the days of the hanging chad. Sothern walked briskly at first, his reedy Ichabod Crane frame fluttering in and out of the scattered ovals of light. The numbness that sometimes replaced the pain in my left leg was wearing off, but I kept up. At least I didn't have to worry about footsteps; the sidewalks were drifted over with dirt, and enough grass had taken root to anchor it. A fresh deposit of dew on the blades plastered my pants cuffs to my ankles and soaked my socks.

We made a few right angles. There was no use memorizing streets; those that were posted belonged to housing developments that hadn't hung around long enough to appear on a city map. I had a general idea of the direction we were going from the lights of the city to the southwest. Their steady reflection off the bellies of the clouds made a neon glow. Every third house was cloaked in an iron grid to keep out squatters, but here and there shivered a tiny flame—orange for kerosene, blue for Sterno. Those, a crowbar, and a pair of bolt-cutters will get you anywhere you need to be after sundown and hold you till dawn. They posed no threat here. The area didn't attract enough foot traffic to tempt predators.

Came a stretch where there was no local illumination at all. The sidewalk ended with a bump; the contractor had run out of money halfway through a pour. Now I navigated as much by the crunching of Sothern's soles on gravel as by sight, and walked on the balls of my feet to keep down my own noise. By now his pace had slowed. Sometimes he paused—maybe to get his bearings in the dark, maybe not.

I stopped when he stopped. I could hear him breathing sporadically, but I was better at holding mine from practice. This happened often enough to make his case that he was being tailed, or thought he was. He was wary suddenly. Maybe I'd lost my touch.

He had manners. He kept off the grass where there was grass, even if five U.S. presidents had done their damage and moved on since anyone had bothered to post a sign. We wound along hypothetical streets and never so much as cut the corner off a burned-out lawn. Now and then a set of headlamps slung light our way, always two or three streets over and never head-on. They didn't belong to our world.

Suddenly he made a square turn; if I hadn't been paying attention I'd have gone right on past.

Now he was approaching a gray-white oblong, a structure only in theory, and one he'd easily have missed himself if he hadn't been there before.

In that instant, I knew where I was.

It was a rounded mass of glazed concrete that might have been baked in a kiln right there on the spot. One day on your way home from work you passed a scalped empty lot, and the next morning the place was there and open for business; and business had been good for a long time. The bay doors had slid up and down to the constant clatter of chain pulleys as traffic moved in and out. The doors were missing now, snagged by scrap rats, making black open spaces like the gaping mouths of a row of ghosts. Die-cast metal letters had spelled the trade name across its front, but those too had gone to scrap, leaving only their hollow outlines: ATLAS MOTORS.

It had had its day of infamy, then faded into a vague image on the edge of recollection, lost in a succession of scandals that had replaced one another with the speed of the twenty-four-hour news cycle. To most locals, it was the place where a woman's body had been found pickled in an oil drum, or maybe where Jimmy Hoffa had stopped for gas on the way to his last supper. For sure it was something bad.

The real story was more colorful.

At its peak, Atlas was the Wall Drug, the Crossroads Mall, the Santa's Workshop of chop shops. *Crain's Detroit Business* compared it to the Ford River Rouge plant: A single set of stolen wheels rolled in one end and emerged two hours later a fleet, stripped, reassembled, and washed in the blood of the lamb with a brand-new Vehicle ID Number and a title that would hold up under a microscope. When it comes to cars, no place compares to the Motor City; none. But Atlas was unique. There, grand theft auto was just an illegal front for a bigger illegal operation.

Under the Kilpatrick administration, it became the main payoff point for City Hall and the Detroit Police Department. Bureaucrats and detective inspectors stopped in for a tune-up and left with cash. Builders, on the other hand, stopped in with cash and left with a city contract.

It couldn't last; that's one reality the grafters never understand. Atlas got off easy. When the mayor finally collided with the federal justice system, the garage skimmed through with a minimum of notoriety: The press found the story just too big to report all the details and muddle the issue. When the FBI took over the city, the management and staff made the best of the confusion and relocated to New Orleans, where the corruption is open and aboveboard.

Sothern's feet scraped cement. I stopped at the edge of the pad that sloped up to the front of the building.

At the top of the grade he spun and faced me. I could just make out his shape against the pale backdrop. I froze. I didn't know how well he could see in my direction, but ducking for cover wasn't an option. A mosquito whined in my ear, landed like a seaplane on a damp spot on the side of my neck, and pierced the skin. I let it drink its fill. After it left, drunken with bloat, the itching burned like a hot spark. I let that go on too.

The city was never more quiet than it was in the thirty seconds we stood without moving; it was as if a frame of film had stuck in the projector. Then he turned back toward the building, and the picture jumped back into motion. He hadn't seen anything.

He spoke suddenly. It was like a firecracker exploding at my feet. But noise was all it was. His voice was too low to make out what he said from just a few yards away.

A shadow shifted inside the building, or maybe it was just a sense that molecules were shifting. Whatever it was, it emerged from the bay far enough to cast a silhouette against the dirty white front of the garage. The figure turned its head slightly, and enough dusty light reflected off it for me to make out the profile. A hand touched his arm and the two turned and started inside.

Just then a car turned a corner a block over. Its lights raked the front of the garage through a space where a building had stood until July 1967. The pair jumped. The woman—I saw now it was a woman—turned her head away. At the same time, Sothern swung square around, and we were face-to-face again; but the glare from behind me must have been too bright and his pupils too slow. When it left and darkness rushed back in, he turned back, but now he was alone. The cuckoo had ducked back into the clock.

I left then. I couldn't risk his giving up and coming back my way. I swung back south, taking it easy on the torn quad and scratching my neck like an old dog with young fleas. After a few blocks I lit a cigarette and let the smoke drift on the humid air.

A pulsar flickered in my brain, then was gone, like all of my high-school French. Just where I'd seen that female profile before would continue to itch long after I'd forgotten all about the mosquito, and something about it was as bad as a pernicious infection.

FIVE

Home.

A lifetime ago, the furniture and décor had been selected with the kind of care usually reserved for casing a bank: pastels or primaries, throw rugs or wall-to-wall, paper or paint. I hadn't any part of it, aside from holding out on my choice of armchairs. The chair's still there, and I suppose so is most of the rest, not counting what had decamped with the other half of the arrangement; cars had shrunk and Ma Bell had metastasized into a dozen different servers since I'd paid any attention to what was on the walls and floor. Function had replaced form. The visitors I entertained wouldn't notice if I'd dug a moat around the living room.

I found a bottle of beer and the makings for a sandwich and had dinner and a show in front of a reboot of a detective series I'd managed to miss throughout its original run. I'd left the remote next to the TV, and just the thought of getting up to switch channels made my leg throb. Anyway the half-baked plot and witless dialogue were an improvement over thinking.

The phone rang. I let it, even though it was on the end table within easy reach; but my patience was no match for the caller's. I picked up, started to say, "A. Walker Investigations," then turned it into a hello in low gear.

The voice on the other end was younger than its owner. Baby

Boomers don't sound like their fathers at the same age; maybe it has to do with not so much shouting on loading docks.

"Mr. Walker, this is Guy Prosper. We haven't met. I'm—"

"I know who you are, Mr. Prosper. Catherine mentioned you once in a Christmas newsletter. Please accept my sympathies on your loss."

"That's very kind of you. It was tough near the end." Something caught in his throat, but he swallowed it. "I suppose you heard about it from a friend."

"We didn't have any friends in common. Frank Usher called."

The silence this time was free of glottal discomfort. When he spoke again his tone was wrapped in an ice-cold sheet. "I didn't know you were in touch."

"Not in twenty years. I'd assumed he was dead. He must be around eighty by now."

"I wouldn't know. She didn't talk about him much, or her late second husband either, just what they both did for a living. She and Usher—she still called him Pym—never spoke, so far as I know. I can't imagine how he found out."

"Sure you do. If she told you about his job."

"I suppose so. I didn't want to say it. You never know who's listening nowadays, do you?" His chuckle sounded like someone crumpling cigarette cellophane.

"People always joke about that. Why, do you suppose?"

"Hard to say. Maybe they hope whoever *is* listening will think they don't mean it and let them alone."

I dropped the subject. "He didn't say much, beyond telling me what happened. The details weren't ironed out yet."

"Naturally, since I'm the one whose responsibility they are." Now his tone was genuine. It hadn't been, even when he'd tried to sound sad. Grief is awkward in our buttoned-up century. It almost always comes across like a tour guide's chant. "I wonder why he told you."

I said I didn't know, but I did. Usher and I had met maybe three times, a third of my life ago, but what had happened in that stretch would figure big in anyone's memoirs.

"Catherine didn't want a funeral, in the usual sense of the term," Prosper said. "I guess not that many do, these days. She's been cremated. The memorial service is on Thursday at six P.M., in Iroquois Heights. The Barnhill and Olson home. Do you know it?"

"Yeah." I kept my tone neutral. The Heights was my favorite suburb after *The Garden of Earthly Delights*. "I'm not sure I can make it, Mr. Prosper."

"Guy, please. We have something important in common, after all. I'd be very grateful if you could come. I have something I'd like to discuss."

I wanted to say I was tied up, but even I couldn't wrestle enough truth into my tone to make it fly; my activities of the evening fell closer to stalker than detective. I said I'd try, repeated my condolences, and cradled the receiver before he could press his case.

My eyes went to the table where a picture used to stand in a kickstand frame; how it had found its way back there after decades in a drawer I couldn't remember. I probably wasn't the first to wonder if the death of an ex-wife meant a man was single again or still divorced.

One of the advantages of being the last dodo in the ecosystem is you don't have to wait your turn in the periodicals section of the Detroit Public Library. Newspapers are like pay phones, branded extinct and forgotten by society, but somehow still available if you have the patience to seek them out.

Bright and early the next morning, stoked on caffeine, tomato juice, and sowbelly, I walked past a queue loitering in front of a computer and browsed among back numbers of the *News* and *Free Press,* draped neatly on wooden dowel rods like towels on a drying rack; the librarians kept them in rotation, the latest up front, the earliest placed in storage before going to microfilm, in hypnotic lockstep like robot servants in a science-fiction story, years after the humans they served were dead and buried.

When I figured I had enough material to start, I carried January through March to a vacant table, stacked them on one end, and sat down to spread them out, one issue at a time.

I ignored the text, concentrating on the photos. I was on my own time, and considering what I charge by the day, I couldn't afford me without cutting corners. Anyway it was a face I was looking for. The name could come later.

It promised all the pitfalls of thumbing through mug books at police headquarters. After a while all the faces looked alike, stick-up artists and holders of public office especially. The visiting celebrities were cut even more obviously from a single bolt: Male and female, they swept past in a blur of cosmetic surgery and plastic smiles. The fact that I was looking for a woman narrowed the search, but after a half hour I had to flex my brain to hang on to what I'd seen last night.

Then I turned a page and dawn broke.

It was in the City section: I knew then that's where it would be, too late to matter.

If I hadn't seen the face in profile I might not have made a connection. That was the angle presented to the photographer as the owner was coming down the steps of the McNamara Federal Building at Michigan and First. Her head was turned toward her lawyer, a tall woman elevated further by five-inch heels and a glistening all-weather coat that came down to mid-calf. The wind that day was coming strong off the river, whipping the counsel's coattails about her legs. The camera caught her client drawing her jaw-length hair back from her face, exposing a slightly bulbous forehead, pug nose, and round chin. Taken one by one there was little in those things to attract, but together they added up to more

than the sum of their parts. It was a face you remembered, even if
you forgot the circumstances.

The usual gaggle of print reporters, Action News standups,
Steadicam operators, and sound crews with their Popsicle mikes
on long sticks swarmed around the pair, moon-walking backwards down the steps with their backs to the cameras. It was the
biggest local story since the discovery of the electric car.

Twenty inches of copy under a two-column head laid out the
details; but the caption summed up the story.

Abelia Hunt had been released on a $100,000 bond following
her arraignment for suspicion of leaking U.S. government secrets
to the press. That victory over the U.S. attorney's push for holding
her without bail was plum advertising for the defense lawyer, Janet
Grasso. A bail bondsman had put up the amount on a ten percent
surety. The defendant's mocha skin looked lighter in the illumination of TV camera reflectors than it had in last night's dusky light,
but there was no mistaking her, not for a trained sleuth like me, or
for that matter a panhandler with cataracts in both eyes.

If it had been Grasso in that garage, I'd have made the connection sooner. Since the item had become a manhunt, she'd been the
go-to guest on every morning talk show in the country, making
appeals to her client to come forward. A hundred PR flacks working around the clock couldn't have gotten her better exposure.

I reassembled the newspaper and returned it to the stack. The
issue had run late in March. I didn't have to browse any further
to remember that the "Hunt for Hunt" had begun a few days later,
when she'd vanished from under the noses of the federal agents
assigned to her surveillance.

That was on April 1. No wonder I'd remembered the date.

She was the product of a common government glitch, known
inside the Beltway as a "Washington Particular"; a clerical worker
necessary for the collation and filing of classified data, but who
was too far down on the totem pole to require top-secret clearance.

That was the bureaucratic black hole through which thousands of reams of super-sensitive material had dropped since Benedict Arnold was a Cub Scout.

Probably it had as much to do with her posting in Detroit, a city long accustomed to being written off by the rest of the world.

The names of undercover agents may or may not have been involved, no one knew for sure with a federal gag order in effect. And just what use Abelia had made of the information, whether to raise her bank balance or blow the whistle or throw the country under the bus just to hear the splat, was up for argument, and would be until she stood trial.

That didn't look as if it would happen soon.

Tourists had seen her in Caracas, Tehran, and Moscow, where she was suspected to have been given political asylum, and Beijing got innings. A sales rep for Walmart spotted her in Dubai, sharing figs with the Taliban; but not even an op-ed writer with a sense of ethics had placed her within a thousand miles of Atlas Motors. That was a secret I seemed to share with Shane Sothern.

SIX

The lot behind the library was a griddle. I climbed into the car long enough to open windows on both sides and found a triangle of shade to smoke in while the steam was escaping. I didn't know if the air conditioner still worked; it had run out of coolant and the kind it used had gone out with the Berlin Wall.

When the sizzling stopped I sealed myself inside and called Barry Stackpole, but even his NASA-quality setup failed to raise a phone number for a Shane Sothern, listed or unlisted, anywhere in the state. I was going to ask for another number, but he told me if I intended to go on using him for tech support we should discuss a retainer and broke the connection. I blamed the heat.

So I bit the bullet and called Russell Feather in Lansing. He'd been hired two administrations ago as liaison between Michigan and Hollywood when the state was offering cash incentives to film here. The terms were the best in the country, so for a while our restaurants and lakefronts resembled a spread in *People*. It couldn't last, and when the administration changed the program was dropped; but the legislature overlooked Feather, who stayed on salary playing Candy Crush in a corner office down the hall from the governor. Tax breaks come and go, but a jack-up is forever.

He answered in the deep guttural of a three-quarter-blood Ojibway: Tonto marinated in peyote oil. His ancestors had misdirected

Cadillac to the site of Detroit when he was looking for the North-west Passage, and it still tickled him.

"Walker, Chief," I said. "I'm still waiting for that call-back from Paramount. When do I get my screen test?"

"Amos! I thought you'd retired when they stopped making key-holes."

"Not yet. I'm after a phone number. It will be unlisted."

"If it weren't, you wouldn't be calling. You know my rates?"

"This one's a minor celebrity by your standards. How about a break?"

"You misdialed, pal. You want Mother Waddles."

"It might turn into something, a second client with deeper pock-ets. We can renegotiate then."

"Either way, that's one expensive cold call."

"This number doesn't belong to the client. I'm hoping he can help me reach the party I'm after."

"Let's start with who it does belong to."

"Gerald Rickey."

"The writer? I think we can do business. Nobody cares about writers. I can give you a package deal, throw in Bret Easton Ellis and Amy Tan."

I told him to hold the Ellis and Tan. We burned five of my not-unlimited phone minutes coming to a figure I could swing by hocking a couple of fillings. He ran a drumroll on some keys, then gave me a number on the Oakland County exchange. I thumbed off and tried it.

"Mr. Rickey's residence."

A female voice with an island lilt. It made me thirsty for a drink with a parasol in it.

"Mr. Rickey, please."

"Your name?"

"It wouldn't mean anything. Tell him it's about Shane Sothern. He's in a jam and I'm trying to get him out."

"Jam?"

"A pickle. A tight spot. A bit of a sticky wicket. Miss, he's in trouble."

"I'll see if Mr. Rickey is in."

She put down the phone. I heard heels on hardwood or possibly tile, a sports broadcast somewhere in another part of the house: the crack of a bat, followed by cheering. If it was a Tigers game the other team must have been up.

Something clicked; an extension line. The baseball game was louder where he was; he spoke up above it. This voice I recognized, from interviews on radio and television, a light uncracked tenor; regular usage in public had kept it from drying out. "This is Gerald Rickey. Who says Shane's in a mess?"

That was one synonym I hadn't thought of. "My name's Amos Walker. I'm a private investigator. He came to me yesterday. He thinks he's being followed."

"You're talking to the wrong person. I'm not one of those writer-adventurers you read about sometimes. I can barely work out the problems I make up myself."

"I wouldn't ask. We parted company before I could find out how to get in touch with him. I can't find a number for him, listed or otherwise. I hoped you could help me."

"How'd you get *my* number? I go to a lot of trouble to keep from being disturbed."

"I'm a good investigator." I'd prepared myself for a curmudgeon. The wrong way to treat one is to be polite.

A beat, then the game cut off. "What's he got himself into this time?"

"I didn't know it was a habit."

"He's quixotic; not necessarily a fault exclusive to youth, but it's more common. He can't seem to develop the shell of objectivity crucial to writing. That's one of the reasons I told him he'll never make it in the field. He tends to take sides, and is always surprised when the other side resents it. I've saved him a lawsuit and a couple of beatings through diplomatic conversation."

I'd never heard *quixotic* out loud before; I assumed Rickey was correct in pronouncing the *x*. "One of the drawbacks of youth, I suppose," I said.

"Not exclusively, although more common. Our society coined the phrase 'old fool' for a reason. You didn't answer my question, Mr. Walker."

"He thinks he's being followed. He's right. I followed him last night after he left my office. More on that later. He says his place was broken into and searched. I believe him. Whatever he's working on, it's got him in over his head and mine."

"That's not vague." Irony dripped off the clear tenor.

"It has to be. Did your housekeeper or whoever I spoke to mention I'm a *private* investigator?"

"That was my secretary," he snapped.

I'd offended him somehow, or maybe he just liked to play the part of the neighborhood crank who wouldn't give a kid back his basketball. Either way a friendly lesson in diplomatic conversation would not be forthcoming. I ran through my card catalogue of tactful rejoinders, but he was too impatient to wait.

"Try the YMCA," he said. "If he's left there, I can't help." The connection went away.

He was a very prolific author. No one ever risked interrupting his routine twice.

Shane hadn't been living at the YMCA; at least not when he was broken into, if that wasn't another of his misdirections. The accommodations were as intimate as a bus station, with traffic to match. I had enough self-esteem to think anyone who had the good sense to come to me for expert help was too smart to leave behind anything useful to an amateur snoop, much less a professional.

But a good detective never overlooks anything.

I ground the starter, swung back north on Woodward, and took Adams to Witherell, where the full name YOUNG MEN'S CHRISTIAN ASSOCIATION was still chiseled in stone over the entrance to the institutional building.

The interior smelled slightly of soap and damp towels, with an undercurrent of mildew too stubborn for even the locally manufactured industrial-strength disinfectant to eradicate. The shallow foyer was simple but sturdy, built to Edwardian-era specifications, with community service plaques on the paneled walls. A clerk stood behind a wooden counter sorting mail into old-fashioned pigeonholes. He was young, but his forehead was advancing through a bush of red hair blown straight out from the scalp, Art Garfunkel style.

"Yes, sir?" Gray-green eyes took me in from the knot of my necktie down to counter level. I was too well turned out for a resident, but not well enough to dine with the mayor.

I handed him the business card I'd selected from the assortment in my wallet. This one read:

> *ADAM WARFIELD*
> *FAMILY LAW*

I told him who I was looking for. He looked at the card front and back, frowning a little, I thought, over the absence of postmodern data: Office address, telephone number with the traditional 313 area code; no cell, no web site, no e-mail address. I'd been carrying it since before Bill Gates had moved out of his parents' basement; so long, anyway, I'd forgotten what Warfield looked like or why I had it. Garfunkel slid it into a polo shirt pocket—for chemical tests later, maybe—picked up the stack of envelopes he'd been holding, and shuffled them. "I remember Sothern. Checked out last month. They don't stay long, as a rule. What's it about?"

"His aunt who raised him is a client. She's in hospice and wants to see him one last time."

He smiled. His dental work was good for a minimum-wage job. "Leaving him a fortune, is she?"

I showed him I took care of my teeth too. As often as someone busted me in the mouth, I kept a dentist on retainer. "Two other guys have had this same conversation." I unshipped my imitation-leather folder and showed him the P.I. license.

"Same initials," he said. "How do I know you didn't print that too?"

"I only keep the cards with my initials; cuts down on the clutter. Anyway, who'd bother with a phony investigator's ticket? The real thing doesn't open any doors." I put it away. When you have to, tell the truth, even if it's too late. "He's the client. We didn't get into whether he has an aunt, rich, terminal, or otherwise. He's in danger, and I don't have any way to get into contact to warn him."

"Is it about the girl?"

It could've been a trap, but I didn't have anything to lose. "Yes."

He leaned forward, folding his arms on the countertop. "He was always taking calls from her on the house phone; from a booth, according to caller ID. I thought they'd all gone out with NSYNC."

"No kidding, they broke up?"

He slid past that. "I heard just enough to know I heard it all before. Shane's a good guy. I don't get chummy with the residents, but he's hard not to like. Maybe you can get through to him; I couldn't, but then when did a friend ever where a woman's involved?" He brought a metal recipe box up from under the counter, thumbed through the cards, and gave me an address in Dearborn. I took it down in my notebook, got out a ten-dollar bill, folding it in my palm out of sight of the surveillance camera mounted in a corner of the ceiling, and shook his hand. When I took mine back the bill was still in it.

"My father's on the GM board," he said when I stared. "He's the kind of man who buys people with chump change. It's why I work here."

I told him I'd remember that, thanked him, and got out from under his scrutiny. The day was still young; I wondered how many more enemies I'd make before quitting time.

SEVEN

Henry Ford wouldn't recognize Dearborn, the town he put on the map.

Why should he? The world laughed when he predicted four lanes of automobile traffic on Woodward Avenue within a decade. Still, the brilliant old bigot would wander around lost among the minarets and Arabic signs on many of the shops. Now it contains the largest Arab population outside the Middle East. Whenever a truck loaded with fertilizer blows up in a busy neighborhood anywhere in the U.S., Dearborn crawls with undercover feds. To them, racial profiling is as American as chop suey.

The address belonged to a Chaldean grill-and-swill in a cinder block box off Oakman, with a painted mural sprawled across the front showing a solemn black-bearded chef turning a lamb on a spit in a grove of palms with a lagoon in the center: A sign with scimitar-shaped letters read OASIS CAFÉ. The artist hadn't stopped at the windows: Clouds and soaring birds of myth covered every pane. You had to know the place in order to find the door. The smell of grease and nutmeg spread all the way down the block. My stomach took up the grumbling refrain when I killed the engine. Breakfast bacon seemed a long time ago.

The painted windows on the second floor would belong to apartments, but places like that don't waste good dining space on staircases. I went down the narrow alley between the building and the discount auto parts shop next door. I had to turn sideways to get past the Dumpster parked outside the kitchen exit. On the other side of the brown steel door, a recorded string section was walloping hell out of something that ought to come with a belly dance.

Behind the café, an outside set of stairs made a diagonal from a concrete slab up to a door on the second story. A gravel parking lot accommodated a half-dozen cars and pickups, some of which would belong to employees. The lunch rush wouldn't start for half an hour. One vehicle, parked at an angle just off the drive from the street that ran alongside the building, was too new for minimum wage. It stuck out like something that was designed not to in any other neighborhood: a dishwater-gray four-door Chrysler with windows tinted too deep for state law.

I stopped inside the alley. The shade felt good in the heat, but it was the dark I wanted. I was jealous of those black windows and the cover they offered to whoever was inside.

If there was anyone inside. It gave the impression of something that had been there a long time, like an empty jar washed up on a deserted beach. Maybe that was the point. In any case it was spotless, in a town where things get dirty just in the act of existing.

It didn't have to mean anything. I couldn't see a plate from that angle, so the car might have belonged to a customer from out of state, stopping to take advantage of the colorful local cuisine; someone on vacation from a job where they frowned on chrome and park decals and clever bumper stickers; an undertaking parlor or a Kingdom Hall. The food might be so good, the service so agreeable, and the company so pleasant, two hours can slip by with a finger to their lips. Not everything's a clue.

Not even when another gray sedan, identical to the first, pulled in next to it.

Seconds later, a man got out of the other car and came around the hood of the second. Not dressed like a professional mourner or pamphlet-peddler, but subdued enough in a gunmetal leather windbreaker, charcoal slacks, and black oxfords. Short sandy hair and a clean-shaven face half obscured by black wraparound sunglasses. Nothing in that; the sun was bright enough to make your head ache. But I had a hunch the eyes behind them were on the prowl. I drew back farther into the alley from instinct.

A tinted window glided down on the driver's side. The man on foot propped a forearm on the roof and bent down to the window. There was a murmur of conversation, vague as the blur of white face inside the car, and then Windbreaker slapped the window post, spun around, and got in behind the wheel of the first car. The motor started as quietly as a lullaby. The car backed into a Y turn and swung out onto the side street. By now the window of the other car was back up, and peace settled over the lot like steam from the ventilator.

But not before I got a glimpse of the first car's license.

I backed away slowly, avoiding movement that would stir shadows, then turned around and retreated to the front of the restaurant. Shane Sothern was sitting on the passenger's side of my front seat.

He was dressed as before; either he had a wardrobe full of *Son of Flubber* outfits or he stood the ensemble in a corner and climbed into it like deep-sea diving gear. I slid in under the wheel. The little patch of shade I'd found to park in had lost ground, but he'd opened the window on his side, leavening the pressure-cooker effect. Still, there was a ripe sting of sweat that wasn't all mine, along with a healthy dose of highly seasoned mutton.

"What'd you do, shinny down the drainpipe?" I said.

"I've been out all day. I stopped in to eat. I saw the car through the window when I went back to use the restroom. I saw yours when I left the place. It seemed a good idea to get out of sight as fast as I could."

"You missed the changing of the guard. I wouldn't worry about the Olsen twins. It's an open tail or they wouldn't be driving regulation wheels with government plates. When they tossed your place they made sure to leave signs they'd been there. One thing those spooks know how to do is intimidate. I think the Justice Department recruits retired mobsters as instructors, just like it smuggled in Nazi scientists for the space program."

"Mr. Walker, what can they possibly want with me? The kind of facts I dig up are public property. Anyone with a library card could find out the same information."

"Even where Abelia Hunt's been hiding out for the last two weeks?"

I pressed the point while he was still taking it in. "You knew before you came to me the Gap boys were trailing you with a brass band. They tend to get careless when they take that route, so it wouldn't be impossible for an amateur to lose them. I had better luck shadowing you to Atlas Motors, but I was taking the basic precautions."

"Atlas Motors, what's that?"

"Before your time, possibly. What's left of the sign is hard to read. That pile of blight on the northwest side. You need to be more careful, Shane. If those jumped-up clerks I saw in the parking lot suspected you'd actually made direct contact with an enemy of the people, they'd be off the job in a white flash and you'd be so lost in the system not even Johnnie Cochran would know where to serve the habeas."

He was still a human mood ring. His shocked pallor warmed to an angry flush. "She isn't an enemy of the people! It's the people she cares about."

"I don't care."

"How can you not? You're an American, aren't you?"

"That plea doesn't go very far in U.S. District Court. You're a material witness in a nationwide manhunt, and I'm the kind of well-intentioned idiot that always gets snagged along with the rest of the small fry in the first news cycle. Have you got a lawyer?"

"No!" He started to say more, then swept both palms out to the sides, erasing an invisible slate. He sucked in a lungful of soggy air and let it out along with a gust of shish kebab; continued in a quieter tone. "Look, I—"

"Stop there. Save the rest for someone who can tell the law to go chase itself."

"But what about you?"

"All part of the plan. Put on your seat belt." I took my eyes off the rearview mirror and twisted the key in the ignition. The big engine throbbed in the soles of my feet.

He took things literally, letting loose a tumble of dead ladybugs when he pulled the passenger's strap from the roller; I don't get many passengers. "Where are we going?"

"Somewhere he won't." I jerked my head toward the mirror on his side, and in it the oyster-colored sedan that had just turned the corner onto our street.

EIGHT

'd either overestimated myself or underestimated the other side; maybe it was a combination of both. In any case the result was the same. I'd been spotted in the alley, and my movements had been suspicious enough to persuade him to desert his post.

Any hope that he'd overlook the car parked in front of the café went out the window when he coasted to a stop directly behind us, next to a fire hydrant.

I didn't wait for him to get out, if that was his plan. I pulled away from the curb and cruised at just above idle. He did the same, and we imitated the O. J. Simpson chase for three blocks. There was no reason to try to lose him. If the Chrysler came with an onboard computer, or if the driver just had a smartphone, he'd made me already from my plate.

So of course I tried to lose him.

Maybe it was because my passenger was breathing like a high-strung horse, hogging all the oxygen in the car, or maybe it was just to break up the monotony. Anyway I put pressure on the foot pedal and wound my way back to Oakman, a four-lane boulevard where the midday traffic was just starting to clot up. My shadow fell back two car lengths, letting a PT Cruiser with a cracked windshield slide in between us. It's all covered in Chapter Six of the manual.

Changing lanes, I swept dust off the fender of a Roadway van, then swung around the corner onto Haggerty without tripping my blinker. Horns brayed. But Chrysler was no rookie. He was back in my mirror before I crossed Manor. He knew what I was up to by then and closed the distance. Shane slumped down in his seat.

"He won't shoot," I said. "It makes for too much paperwork."

"Let's just get away from him, okay? Even if it's just for an hour."

"Sounds sensible. We can use the fresh air."

"Fresh—" He slammed shoulder-first into the door on his side.

I made the horseshoe turn on the outside edge of the radials and braked against the curb, hard enough to send the gas walloping around inside the tank.

Chrysler didn't panic. Half a block past us, he pulled over and slid to a stop alongside a young maple dying in a box on the sidewalk. We were facing different directions; the natural thing to do was burn rubber and hope to shake him while he was turning, but he hadn't been trained to expect the obvious. He waited.

We'd stopped beside a check-cashing place with a neon dollar sign for the S in its name. I popped open my door. "Let's hoof it."

Shane caught up with me inside the building. There a clerk with a jaw that would support a flagpole watched us through bulletproof glass, both hands out of sight under the counter, where the pistol would be. I beat him to the draw with my ID folder. It was back in my pocket even faster; the badge wouldn't fool a child. "Back door!" I barked.

He threw his big chin at a steel slab with a sign that said FIRE EXIT ALARM WILL SOUND. "Stick your fingers in your ears."

"Perfect." I crossed the floor in four strides and gave the crash bar a shove. They heard the clanging in Chicago. I swung around, intercepted Shane in hot pursuit, grabbing him by the shoulders and riding him like a toboggan all the way back to the entrance.

We were standing against the wall next to the door when an

athletic-looking character in a gray windbreaker and black shades loped in, spotted the fire exit, and broke into a gallop; he never turned his head our way. He looked so much like the man he'd relieved back at the Oasis I couldn't have picked either one out of a lineup. We were outside before the metal door drifted shut, and halfway back to the Cutlass while the glass front door was still closing.

I put three turns between us and the abandoned Chrysler, then slowed down. "That only works when they don't travel in pairs," I said. "You never know when a vehicular tail will turn into a footrace."

"You actually like this, don't you?"

"Admit it: You're feeling pretty good yourself right now."

"Maybe a little. But where do we go from here?"

I told him.

He gawked, then shook his head hard enough to knock loose his glasses. He slid them back up his nose.

"We can't! I only went there last night to find out if she needed supplies. I was being careful, and still I led you right to her. What if that man back there wasn't the only one following us?"

"Rest easy. That wasn't the only fire exit in town."

Not everything looks better in daylight. At least at night you can't see vacant lots turned into city dumps, read obscenities misspelled in Day-Glo on alley walls, witness meth deals conducted as openly as delivering pizza. There wasn't a straight line or a right angle for blocks. Roofs sagged, chimneys leaned; every porch was seceding from the rest of the house. The air smelled of sodden ash, the signature scent of an arson investigation in progress. Ten minutes from the skyscrapers downtown, Detroit bore every sign of a civilization in hospice.

I parked two streets over from Atlas; if our pet spy managed to pick up our trail it would stop at the car. Shane watched as I took the Chief's Special in its holster from behind the false wall of the glove compartment and snapped it on my belt. I dropped my shirttail over it.

"Do you think we'll need that?"

"When I don't have it is when I need it most."

Not everyone was away at work. Natives in undershirts drank beer on their stoops and in plastic lawn chairs, watching us change the routine in the neighborhood. It was too hot to do anything about it.

A narrow street fenced off from extinct railroad tracks was all that separated the residential zone from the commercial. Once past that we went unobserved the rest of the way to the deserted garage. Approached from behind, it looked like one of those domes where MDOT stored salt to spread on winter roads. That side wasn't tiled. Yellowed mortar crumbled like cornbread and made piles on the ground. Pillars of bald tires and dead batteries and heaps of empty plastic bottles lined the blank wall. The earth was stained orange with rust, but scrapyard scavengers had made off with the metal.

There were no out-of-place cars in sight, no suspicious commercial vans, no helicopters black or otherwise. The romance had worn off, leaving only soggy heat.

We circled around to the front, me trailing Shane with the caution of experience. A few yards short of the empty bays he held up and stuck a hand behind him, signaling me to stop. I waited while he identified himself in his clear light baritone. I'd almost forgotten there was anyone to hear it, the area was that desolate.

There was no answer, no sound at all apart from the droning traffic on the freeway closest to us. He called again, waited; looked at me. I nodded and we walked the rest of the way up the concrete ramp. The revolver was in my hand. I didn't remember drawing it.

Inside was the kind of twilight reserved for windowless buildings at noon on a bright day. The place smelled dank; all traces of oil and grease and scorched radiator had gone the way of the previous tenant. That left the three of us alone, counting the dead man.

The human mind is funny. Under some circumstances, the first thought is the right one. This wasn't one of those circumstances.

The corpse at our feet belonged to the federal agent we'd ditched minutes before: Same gray clothes, same dark hair in a 1950s cut, same black shoes with waffle treads, suitable for driving or walking on hard tiles without making noise, the identical dark glasses, not quite wrapped around his face now, with one side bow loose and drawing a black arc under his left cheekbone to expose an eye as big as a golf ball; they look bigger than you think when they start from the socket. It stuck out almost as far as his tongue.

But it wasn't the same man.

Just to be sure I leaned down and touched his cheek. It had grown cool in the shade. There hadn't been time enough for that, even if he'd figured out where we were going and beat us to the spot. It was his twin, the one who'd gotten out of his car to report to his partner during the surveillance handoff outside the café in Dearborn.

There wasn't any need to check for a pulse. Even apart from the loss of body heat, the angry ligature around his neck was the purple-black shade of no oxygen reaching his lungs again, ever; the cord was buried so deep in the flesh only the twist of thin filament the killer had wound around his hands was visible. He lay on his side, his half-zipped jacket gapped open just enough to show the square-handled automatic in an open-toed sheath under his left arm. It hadn't done him any good with both hands involved trying to keep himself from strangling to death.

Right-hand holster. If the two were in fact twins, that might make his partner a lefty. That was of no significance then or later. There's no practical pattern to how one thinks in times of shock.

Not that what I was feeling qualified as shock compared to Shane Sothern. When I straightened up, his face was grayer than the bare cement walls and his teeth were chattering. I gave him a gentle slap on the cheek. You don't smack a trauma case hard. It can send him the rest of the way over the edge, same as waking a sleepwalker.

In retrospect, I should have remembered I was holding a gun in that hand.

The barrel left a pink welt clear across his left ear and the weight of the piece knocked him off balance. I had to throw my arms around him to keep him from joining the dead man on the floor.

In any case, it was one of those rare times when a good stiff jolt does the trick. He swept a palm to his cheek, brought it away to inspect it for blood—there was none—shook his head, and gaped at me with the expression of a child who's been spanked for something he didn't do.

"Sorry." I let go, jerked straight his corduroy coat, and holstered the .38. "If you're not up to it, find a place to sit down while I check the place out."

"I'm okay. She might be hurt."

She was probably worse; but if I had to slap him again I might as well wait.

As it turned out, we had the place to ourselves. A half-wall with a piece of pegboard attached separated us from the adjoining bay. There was no sign of Abelia Hunt there, apart from a sleeping bag, greasy fast-food sacks, and a dozen or so empty water bottles dumped in the old grease pit. An organized person, our fugitive from justice; once a clerk, always a clerk. We didn't look for toilet facilities. She would likely take care of business camper-style, bagging up waste and scooping out a hole in the dirt outside after dark. How long she'd been doing that in that spot, maybe Shane could tell me later, when and if it mattered.

Four empty steel sockets, all that remained of the hydraulic lift, had resisted all the efforts of even our talented local scrap hounds. They were stuffed to the tops with trash.

There was a built-in workbench of unplaned pine, the top scarred all over from banging on fenders and frozen pistons, burned by battery acid, and stained with every color of lubricant, with rectangular holes where the metal drawers had been removed.

I probably wasn't the first to make that discovery, or of the missing hoist, or for that matter to look for it. Someone had scouted out the place and concluded there was nothing for the scroungers to come back after. In that neighborhood, there was no reason for anyone ever to visit; even the homeless had their choice of more comfortable accommodations in our abundance of vacant houses. I wondered how many accomplices Abelia had in her flight from justice, or if my companion had more talents than he seemed to advertise. He'd managed to slough off a serious case of shock without even rolling up his sleeves. Then again, I'm not qualified to pass verdict. It had been too long since anything had given me a case of my own.

We went back to the corpse. Why, except to confirm we hadn't imagined it? It sure wasn't to do more detecting. In another life I'd have frisked the body for whatever it could tell me; in another life I had. But if he was any kind of field agent his pockets wouldn't turn up anything more informative than an official ID with his name and whatever alphabet agency had employed him. There wasn't anything I could do with it.

We hadn't imagined the corpse. It lay there as fixed in its spot as if the place had been built around it.

Nothing else to report, apart from some overlapping footprints in the dust and loose grit on the floor. Sherlock Holmes would spend a lot of time on them, and provide a description of all the owners, down to their body mass index, the length of their stride, and whether they preferred their eggs over easy or sunny-side up. I hadn't that much leisure; not if I was going to get us both out of there before Penn came barging in to find out what had happened to Teller. And not unless I could scare up a client with a bankroll big enough to make it worth the risk.

NINE

Outside, clouds were shoving in from Canada, threatening either a storm or the suffocation that comes with a low ceiling and high humidity, tight as the seal on a pickle jar. I could feel pressure building already; I hoped it was the weather. It was still bright enough to see a tire track in a bald spot in the grass a few doors down from Atlas Motors, the tread marks as sharp as etched steel. That had to be the only fresh rubber for blocks around. A good forensics team could likely match it to those behind the Dearborn café, and the detectives could speculate that someone, possibly the murderer, had fled the scene in the feds' car.

And, being detectives, would speculate that killer, thief, and Abelia Hunt were one and the same.

We dawdled just long enough to confirm no one was around who might tie us to the scene. Then we retraced our steps to the Cutlass. A backyard dog we'd somehow managed not to alert earlier flung itself against a wire fence, yammering like all the hounds of hell. We didn't jump more than a foot. The fighting pit bull, half-starved and pumped full of steroids, is a more appropriate Detroit mascot than a Tiger or a Lion, and has a better season record.

I drove a route that seemed aimless but wasn't. Soon we passed a parked gray Chrysler with a U.S. plate, a ten-minute walk from the garage, which exploded my original theory. It was the plate

I'd seen leaving the Oasis. *Two* well-kept vehicles visiting Atlas at the same time ought to have attracted interest; but then so would a Neighborhood Watch sign. Shane seemed to have reached the same conclusion. Anyway he didn't ask any questions.

Back at the office, I locked us in and broke the seal on the Christmas bottle I'd put in the safe for special occasions: weddings, anniversaries, cadavers.

"I don't really drink." Shane frowned at the brimming pony glass I'd put on his side of the desk.

"Start." I sat back and put mine away Cowboy Channel fashion; if using both hands qualifies. Anyway what I spilled didn't burn a hole in the veneer. It was good Scotch. I refilled my glass, this time a little down from the top. The shaking had slowed.

Shane set his down after one sip, wrinkling his nose. "Should we call the police?"

"They wouldn't have it five minutes before Washington rolled in and offered to send us both to the Milan federal pen for harboring a traitor. From there it's a short hop to lethal injection."

"Michigan doesn't have the death penalty," he said, as if that were the issue.

"The feds don't pay attention to that. When one of their own goes down they're the last court of appeal."

"I'm not harboring anyone."

"Not anymore. She's your bargaining chip now. They'll put up the needle if you tell them where she is."

"But I don't *know* where she is!"

"Let's hope they don't believe you. Still got that money?"

He scrambled to retrieve the wad of bills. I counted them and locked them in the safe. Then I picked up the phone and got a number from Information.

"Grasso Legal Services."

A female voice, cultured and steel-smooth. I dropped Abelia Hunt's name and another voice came on.

"This is Janet Grasso." This one was less flinty, more aris-
tocratic: One of those melodic Kentucky bluegrass accents that
come with tall green drinks and picture hats. It matched the tall
slender woman who'd accompanied Abelia into the federal building before she vanished. I'd heard the voice on the radio and TV
whenever the manhunt threatened to go stale.

I gave her my name and said I had a line on her client's where-
abouts, but my contact needed representation.

"Mm-hm." But she took down my professional references and
asked me to hold. Thirty-two bars into "Delta Dawn" she came
back on, more honey in her tone. "I don't suppose your contact has
a name."

"Not over the phone, and I don't know when I can present him
in person. When Uncle Sam comes around I want to tell him I'm
lawyered up and go climb a flagpole."

"Is that all?"

"For now."

She didn't pause. "I'm flying to Washington tonight. I'll call
when I get back. If you don't have a name for me then, I'll give
yours to Uncle."

I thanked her and hung up. Shane said, "I can't afford you *and*
a lawyer."

"You won't have to. She needs the win. Our end is to deliver a
twofer: her client and whoever killed a federal agent."

"How can we do that?"

"If I knew, we wouldn't need Grasso and her trip to D.C.; part
of which time I'll spend finding out how you got into this mess
and how I'm going to get you out. Me, too, if there's time." I took
the receiver off the hook, laid it on the blotter, and turned off my
cell. "Start talking."

He did. It sounded like something out of a Gerald Rickey novel:
An "anonymous source" had put Sothern on to Abelia Hunt's hide-
out just days after she fell off the earth. I'd chased too many of

those ghosts to waste sweat pumping him for a name. In any case I had a hunch who it was.

The opportunity had been too good for Kid Scoop to pass up; Barry Stackpole would've been on it like ketchup on a French fry. Shane had followed the directions and also the instructions about how to avoid dragging a train behind him.

The meeting took place inside Atlas Motors. Abelia spoke around a crispy chicken sandwich and two bottles of water, a housewarming gift from the visitor. Shane wasn't sure why she confided in him, but I was: His profile was so low a government spook wouldn't trip over it. The rest was pure personality. Even a fugitive sought in every country in the world would find it hard not to spill her guts to such a living embodiment of Tickle Me Elmo, and he in his turn was just the kind of sap who would accept the story without testing it for leaks. It was a match made in millennial heaven.

And it seemed too good to be true, but I accepted it as a working hypothesis. I hadn't anything else to go on except a tire tread that in a little while would be mud mixed with road salt.

"She's been made the victim of a monstrous cover-up," he said. "She came across evidence that our government has been conducting illegal surveillance on American citizens on a grand scale: interfering with mail delivery in order to record the names of their contacts, tapping their phones, bugging their homes and offices. She tried going to the media, but they treated it as a joke. Whether they're honestly doubtful or part of the conspiracy, she doesn't know. Anyway it was those documents she copied and shared with them that got her in trouble.

"And there's more she hasn't shared," I said. "As reasons go to join her in the bear trap, that one trumps the Galahad complex. You want the material to spice up the story you're going to peddle."

His color came and went. "What do you think I am?"

"Simmer down. There isn't a newshound in the country who'd

pass up the chance. She must know she can't hide out forever. There are four major agencies that have nothing to do but root out threats to national security. Now, with one of their own murdered, they'll come shooting."

"She knows that—about her original position, I mean. She intends to surrender herself eventually, or she did. But not before she has a chance to get her story out. That's where *I* come in, no matter what you think of my reasons."

"This is where you go out. Now."

His chin wobbled. "I can't! She's counting on me to—"

"—go down with her in flames. You need to brush up on your history. Sometimes these hot-button political rebels go to jail or worse; usually not, because once they make breaking news they acquire a following: Pesky folk with picket signs and pro-bono lawyers, bad for the public image and another clog in the criminal justice system. It's the helping hands that get nailed to the cross."

"Give me back my money."

I opened the safe, took it out, and slid it across the desk, dealing myself two hundred off the top first. "Kill fee," I said. "Rotten compensation for bending my credit with the lawyer, but I'm one of those marginal types I was talking about. I might need her in my own corner."

A lip got chewed. Then a head got shaken. He pushed the stack back my way with both hands. "I've got nowhere else to go. That's as close to an apology as you'll get from me."

Part of me wanted to punch his face through the back of his head. The rest of me was glad to see there was a sliver of steel in all that post-grad mush. I put a couple of bills in my wallet and returned the rest to the safe. When I swiveled back his way, his glass had half emptied itself. I refilled mine, topped his off, and sat back, cradling my drink in both hands. "Okay, let's concentrate on how the party in the Foster Grants found his way to Atlas Motors."

"Maybe we didn't lose him after all."

"Not the same spook. They weren't really twins; not identical, anyway. Just two recent trainees from the same dye lot, and probably the same barber."

"I'm sure no one followed me any of the times I went to see Abelia—oh." He went red.

"We'll skip last night," I said. "You went through the rudiments of shaking a tail, but I'm as good as my advertising. What are the chances someone in the place you're living now tipped him off? He handed off the stakeout to his relief plenty quick for someone with a hot lead. If he'd passed it on, his partner wouldn't have had any reason to follow us. It wouldn't be the first time a team player decided to pitch, hit, and run the bases all by himself for the sake of the sports section."

"I don't see how anyone could have told him anything. I've only been there a couple of weeks."

"The desk jockey at the YMCA said you took at least one call from a woman while you were camping out there. Was the woman Abelia, and did she call you again at the Oasis?"

His face bled out. I reminded myself to play poker with him someday. I nodded.

"We'll go with that, for what it's worth, which is enough. We're not prepping for your day in court. If you spoke on a landline, there was an extension, and if it was on a cell, someone eavesdropped. When they turn the space above a hash house into apartments, they rarely waste money on the materials."

"I only use my cell. She called from a pay phone."

I knocked the top off my glass, let the liquid pool in my throat for a moment before committing it to my stomach. "Now let's move on to whether we're helping a killer evade justice."

"No. Absolutely not. You'll have to take that on faith. No one who would do what she did for the reasons she had would commit murder."

"You're assuming the reasons she gave you were the reasons she had."

"What could she possibly have gained, apart from bringing attention to American citizens that their liberties are being taken away? Whatever else she might be holding back—and I'm not saying she did—what she gave to the press was dynamite, with no money exchanged or expected. She's a patriot, not a traitor."

"So was Nathan Hale." I picked up the landline and dialed another number I knew as well as my own.

"Who are you calling?" He looked alarmed.

"Chill out. It's not nine-one-one."

The voice that answered was a cross between a pitch for the Republican Party and someone who doesn't really care how important your call is; it had all the personality of a P.A. announcement. The owner of the machine was still using the recording that came with it. "Barry, it's Walker. I'm at the office."

I cradled the receiver, picked up my glass, and met his blank look with a grin.

"The code in the old days was to let it ring ten times; but Ma and all the Baby Bells don't let you do that now. He'll call back in a couple of minutes. Or not. You never know whether he's being paranoid or out stalking someone, disguised as Mother Teresa."

"Who is he, some kind of spybuster?"

"Not just spies. Tell him what you want busted, it's busted. You said Abelia wants press. If she'd called Barry first, she might not be on the run."

He was still working on that when the phone rang.

TEN

Fairlane—named for the old Ford estate—is one of the oldest shopping malls in the country, and one of the most controversial. Some years back the local black community staged a boycott based on accusations of racial discrimination, but thanks to a lot of gassing by politicians and self-appointed activist leaders and the usual apologetic bromides, the shops and soft-pretzel stands survived.

There's a parking lot for each point on the compass, and a man could wander the concrete landscape for a week trying to remember where he'd parked; on any given day, bag-carrying patrons can be seen playing Marco Polo with their remote keys, looking for their cars.

The veteran shoppers—the well-to-do ones, anyway—stake permanent claim on the lot outside Saks. The spot a customer selects says as much about his credit rating as the car he parks. I chose JCPenney.

When we got out, the air was as heavy as atomic weight. Even the gulls were afraid to land on the steaming asphalt. Two minutes after we entered the store, the conditioned air wrapped us in wet cellophane.

The food court sprawled across the groin where the corridors intersected. Mrs. Fields, Fatburger, Taco Bell, and Sbarro turned it into a bazaar of sizzling griddles, treacly music, and cross-conversation. The place smelled like fried everything.

Barry wasn't hard to spot, if you knew what to look for. When he goes sub rosa he never bothers with wigs and putty noses. Those things only work in the movies and on the stage, a mile from the audience with the lights just so. The trick is to wear clothes no one looks at twice; in this case the bright blue coveralls of mall maintenance and ROY scripted across the breast pocket. People who noticed him at all never got as far as the face. He was plowing his way through a Subway meatball sandwich and iced tea in a plastic cup the size of a silo.

The menu wasn't necessarily part of the disguise. When the all-you-can-eat places see him coming they lock their doors, turn off the lights, and hold their breath until he leaves. By rights he should weigh three hundred pounds; but he's worn the same 170 on a five-eleven frame since Nixon came back from China. When he's on the scent of a blackleg or a bomb-chucker or a holder of any public office, he can forget to eat for days, and sits down only when standing draws too much attention.

Barry was just ham enough this time to stiff his barber, lay off shampoo, and let his sandy hair grow into a matted mop. Some attempt had been made at chin-stubble, but since he never had to shave more than twice a month, he'd settled for a couple of patches of silvery down. That was the only gray north of his collar, and possibly everywhere else; we don't hang out in locker rooms.

He didn't look up as we crossed the court, but he'd come up with a signal for when it was okay to join him. He stretched a leg under the table and scraped the opposite chair a couple of inches into the aisle. I could never remember which leg was flesh and bone and which the product of modern medical engineering. I pulled the chair out the rest of the way and sat. Shane liberated one from a vacant table nearby and perched on the edge of the seat with his hands in his lap. Barry spun a bag of barbecue chips his direction.

"You don't have to eat any," he said. "Just rummage around inside and pretend. You want to look like someone who eats in these dumps, not like you're here to buy a phony Rolex."

Shane dove in, crunching with what sounded like an enviably full set of teeth. I wondered when he'd eaten last; wondered when *I* had, come to that. I helped myself to a Cinnabon wallowing in a crumple of paper sack and made introductions.

"Long-term stakeout, from the looks of things," I said. "You look like a high-school production of *Our Town*."

"It all comes off today, jackass. The guy I was watching got stood up and left a perfectly good falafel on his table. It was the no-show I was after. By now he's halfway across the Gulf of Aden with a satchel full of high-grade Colombian coke."

Shane slid even farther forward. "Mr. Walker says you're a journalist. You sound like a policeman."

"They put slugs like that in jail. I put 'em in print. And stop talking like a con planning a jailbreak: Speak up. Anyone might think you've got secrets to share. All the successful military coups begin in a public place with strangers all around."

Shane sat back and made a try at a grin. He raised the volume. "Sort of like 'The Purloined Letter.'"

"Literate." Barry looked at me. "Your clientele's improving. Next thing I know you'll be bumming around with Dame Edna."

"What happened to the falafel?"

"It's a sin to waste food. What's so important I had to sit on this torture rack till my ass felt like my tin leg?"

I gave him what we had, Shane piping in from time to time to refine the details. Barry was right about the venue. None of the diners within possible earshot knew we existed. The ceiling was high enough to swallow Tarzan's yell. Barry ate, drank, and looked more interested in the dinner than the show. To look at him was to feel sorry for the sap stuck listening to a couple of bores: all part of the camouflage.

When we got to the dead man in the garage he sat back and wiped his hands on a coarse brown napkin. One of them had only two fingers and a thumb, but all that and the business with the leg had happened before he'd learned how to be invisible.

"A murder with only one suspect wouldn't make a game of Clue," he said when we finished. "It was the whistle-blower with the rope in the chop shop."

"Not a rope," I said. "More like fishline."

Shane's eyes flared bright blue behind his glasses. "Where would she learn to do that?"

"*Sesame Street.* Amos, is this kid for real?"

"I overslept. By the time I got up all the good clients were taken."

"What you're saying is ridiculous," Shane said. "What's more it's slander. The whole reason she's in trouble is she wanted to expose an injustice, not commit one of her own."

Okay." Barry started to lean forward and fold his arms on the table, then caught himself and made more rude noises with his straw. "Let's give her the benefit of almost no doubt at all and say somebody else squiffed the fed. Where'd she go, and how did she? Run out while Mr. X was choking him to death, or throw in with X afterward for the ride, or get snatched? And what are we supposed to do about any of that?"

I said, "That's the question we came here to ask. Once some derelict sniffs out those fast-food leftovers in the garage and stumbles over James Bond, Junior, in come the black op boys in Kevlar, looking for blood. We need to find her before they do, if just to get her side of the story."

"You knew the answer to that one before you came: You won't. You're outgunned."

"Custer was outgunned. We're in the Roman Coliseum smothered in Purina Lion Chow."

"It'll help to know which cat we're up against. If it's the FBI it's one thing, CIA another; Department of Homeland Security something else again. They've all got methods they don't share with their friends on the playground. And the amount of manpower goes up in the order I named them. You're asking for a battle plan and you don't even know who you're fighting."

A boy carrying a plastic crate stopped at the table next to ours to clear away the debris. Barry swung the sack back around and foraged among the crumbs until the boy moved on.

"Think that kid worries about getting old?" Barry said. "Regrets the choices he made?"

"Stuff just as bad, probably, for him. Are we getting maudlin in our dotage?"

"Just taking stock." He assembled his trash. "I'll see what I can find out. It's going to mean using a series of Chinese boxes so it doesn't get traced back to me. When it comes out on your end—if it comes out—the first I hear of it better not be on CNN."

"Goes without saying."

"Say it anyway."

I said it. He looked at Shane, who said, "I'm a print journalist, or hope to be. The networks are the enemy."

"Okay," Barry said. "So I'm paranoid. It's an asset that's paid for itself a hundred times over. It better be good for one more round. This could be my last time in the Coliseum. Forget anything you've heard about the Bill of Rights; Washington renegotiates that contract every few years. This one needs to count so I'll have something pleasant to think about on Death Row. You, too," he said. "Both of you. And I'll do us all a favor. I won't move on this for forty-eight hours. Maybe everything will sort itself out by then. But remember the monkeys."

"Remind me," I said.

"'See no evil'—this crew learned how to ensure that as far back as Valley Forge. 'Speak no evil'—the conspiracy nuts took all the teeth out of that one. Nobody pays attention. 'Hear no evil,' now; that's the one keeps them up nights. Silence is their stock-in-trade. Take it away and they're just another bunch of government bureaucrats sucking on the tit. The last thing you want to be is the monkey in the middle."

Traffic on the on-ramp to the Southfield Freeway stood still at that hour. There were eight cars ahead of us waiting their turn in the Cuisinart. While we sat, the clouds came down to the top of the radio antenna, a true lamp black. The wind came up and brought the iron smell of rain. I switched on the radio long enough to hear the orgasmic forecast (the more severe the better), broken up as it was by crackles of charged nitrogen, then turned it off. A lot of households were going to miss *Gilligan's Island* tonight.

The first drops smacked the windshield and flattened out like thumbprints; by the time we caught up with the hometown stream between shifts at Ford, we might have been driving through the whale tank at SeaWorld. The wipers whooshed and thumped like idiots, signifying nothing. I knew how they felt.

All this time Shane was quiet. Then: "Your friend has a persecution complex."

I shouted above the rain thudding the roof. "There's nothing complex about a prosthetic leg and a steel plate in your skull."

"You told me it was gangsters did that."

"That's what the headlines said. He wasn't in shape to write them at the time."

He changed the subject. People generally do when it's that one. "Where are we going?"

"I'm taking you home."

"Won't that be the first place they look?"

"It would be the first place *I* looked. If you're not there, they'll assume you're the killer and drop every other line of investigation.

Also you're better off meeting them there than on the street. Cops—*all* cops, federal, vegetable, or mineral—don't like open spaces, so they try to contain the situation with bullets. They're more housebroken indoors."

A flatbed semi carrying fifteen tons of steel pipe passed us, enveloping the car in propeller wash. I fought the wheel and slowed down to avoid hydroplaning in its wake. I sensed Shane's panic. It wasn't the thought of crashing that triggered it.

"They're not the Mongol Horde," I said. "They prefer asking questions to cleaning up after a corpse. If they take you in, use your phone call. Don't forget you've got a crackerjack lawyer, one who knows the Hunt case better than Abelia. She may tell you to keep your mouth shut, which means they'll threaten to put you in custody. If she's as smart as I know she is, she'll make a deal: A full statement in return for your release. It's Abelia they want. Washington doesn't award appropriations based on the small fry the agencies snag in the net."

"I hope you're right."

So did I, but I didn't say it. The rain wasn't letting up and I had ditches to avoid. Not to mention a funeral to prepare for.

ELEVEN

The site chosen for the memorial service commanded the corner of Spring and Seminole Streets in Iroquois Heights, one zoned residential, the other part of the business district. The house had represented the worst of Edwardian taste for a century, with octagonal turrets and bay and bow windows and beach-striped awnings sticking out in all directions like Shane Sothern's hair. At one time the hexagonal shingles, oak siding, and porches had been painted in a variety of pastels, but recent owners had switched to a leaden gray, saving time and money to replace the jigsaw arrangement of roofs. Still the place stood out among the neighboring renovations like a parade float. A sign pegged in the lawn read BARNHILL–OLSON FUNERAL HOME in black scrolling on white enamel.

I knew the place, although I'd never visited it. The director had paid a bundle to a City Hall fixer for the contract to bury indigents and first dibs at expired public servants fit for a splendid lying-in-state. That was then, this is now. An entirely different crowd had committed its well-upholstered behinds to the leather-and-horsehair upholstery downtown, but a machine is a machine whether it runs on gas or electric current.

The first party to occupy the place of honor in the bay window on the Seminole Street side was the man who had built the house, a stove-manufacturing magnate named Kronkhammer who blew out his brains during the Panic of 1873 with the Frontier Colt he'd carried while prospecting for iron in the Upper Peninsula; or maybe it was copper. Before his death, the old claim-jumper had been left in the dust by an early Michigan governor, who founded a syndicate with his cronies to buy up all the land in the area for about twenty-five cents an acre and sell to the developers at five dollars a pop.

I didn't know if either Barnhill or Olson was still running the business, if a son or sons had taken it up, or if it's just that a new sign is an unnecessary expense. This one had been there since Prohibition, when like so many other local enterprises the mortuary moonlighted in the liquor trade. The big double side doors admitted barrels of sour mash as easily as coffins.

Catherine Stokes (for a little while Catherine Walker) had never starved for friends. She sparkled in their company, as opposed to the dim glow she cast in private. The parking lot had overflowed into the street: glistening sedans, sporty coupes, luxury SUVs, and Hummers micro-parked in the slots and lining the curb bumper-to-bumper. She'd moved up in the world since divorcing a private operative without life insurance or a credit rating. I'd stopped resenting her for that; it was the right thing to do for who she was. My prospects hadn't improved in the years since.

I parked down the block where the regular commuters left their vehicles and got out, checking for mud on my cuffs. It was the suit I keep in dry-cleaners' plastic for occasions of state.

A post office van stopped on the corner to service a bank of mailboxes on a post. A puddle left over from yesterday's downpour reached almost to its hubs. The air smelled clean and scrubbed and the sky was bright enough to rewind my hangover back to the beginning. Obsequies that take place in fair weather are more depressing than most. You always feel sorry someone missed such a nice day.

I checked my phone for missed calls. It was blank. I had Shane's number now. I'd called him twice already and he wasn't in jail either time. There was nothing on the air or in the morning paper about the body in the garage. That might be the situation until he got ripe; maybe not even then, in that part of town, although sooner or later someone would spot his car and frisk the place for blocks around.

Which might explain how he'd stumbled on Atlas Motors. An intelligence agent with intelligence would pick a place of desolation to mount a search; that would account for why the car hadn't been parked by the garage. He'd have struck out on foot, looking for a frightened young woman and not an assassin with a noose. But for me there was nothing to be done until Abelia Hunt showed or the feds turned up the heat.

The foyer was the standard arrangement of thick mauve carpet, indirect lighting, a guest book spread open on a lectern, organ music piped in from Bach's rec room, and a black menu board with white snap-on letters:

CATHERINE STOKES SERVICE 6 P.M. VIEWING ROOM B.

She'd gone to her maiden name after she buried her second husband, and hadn't married Guy Prosper, the man she'd been living with for a dozen years.

I was a few minutes early, but this room, paneled in walnut and fairly large, was filling up. Couples and groups conversed in murmurs. I was almost the only man in a jacket and tie, but in our drive-in society I was used to that. I'd just wanted to get some wear out of the outfit before styles changed.

A blue-and-gold-enameled urn stood on a pedestal table on velvet cloth. She'd have appreciated that center spot.

An easel displayed a recent head shot blown up to poster-size occupied an easel next to the speaker's podium. She'd aged well, even allowing for possible Botox and touch-ups: Some wrinkles, the merest beginning of a jowl, and her hair, which I'd seen auburn, strawberry with blond highlights, and once a startling platinum after a salon disaster, fell to her shoulders like spun silver. The eyes, not quite olive but close, still tilted away from the nose, giving a sad cast to the face even when it was smiling. I saw she'd gone ahead and put veneers on her teeth. We'd fought about that.

It struck me then that she was dead. It's always like that in a mortuary; on your way there you thought you were just paying respect to someone who didn't mean very much to you anymore, and once inside, the picture and the receptacle and the mawkish music struck you like a blow to the heart. Not all the memories are bad, and even the bad ones aren't as bad as they'd seemed.

The last one wasn't good. She'd come to me to ask if her then-husband had hired me to stalk her and the man she was having an affair with. It had turned out to be more complicated than that. The man, who introduced himself to me as Frank Usher—she knew him as Edgar Pym—was a CIA field agent who'd taken up with her in order to spy on the husband, a fellow employee who planned to quit the Company and was probably peddling its secrets.

Catherine never had been especially lucky. Both her new men had actually turned out to be a step down from a struggling independent detective.

The husband was dead, one of the growing number of murder victims in my personal collection, and after so many years I'd supposed Usher had moved on to that Checkpoint Charlie in the sky. Even back then he'd been close to sixty, a gray little man you wouldn't remember five minutes after he stuck you up on the street. Which is the kind of recruit spymasters prefer. When he'd called the office to tell me about Catherine, it had taken me a moment to dredge him up.

"Thank you so much for coming."

I jumped a little. Some detective I was. I'd been too tangled in the past to notice another man in a suit offering his hand.

I took it. He had a solid grip and enough confidence in it not to twist my fingers together like pipe cleaners. "Mr. Prosper?"

"Guy, please. We have something important in common. I've seen your picture. It's one of the few things she never threw away. She wasn't much of a pack rat."

"She wanted a house she could clean with a leaf blower."

His laugh was quiet, genuine. He was younger than Catherine, a well-set-up man of fifty. The suit looked out of place. He'd built a successful contracting firm from the ground up, and would look more natural in coveralls than he did in the suit: His head was made for a hard hat. The hair was crisp gray, thinning at the temples, and the long square-jawed face was tan and creased around the eyes by sun and wind.

"Is he here?" I said.

He knew who I meant.

"I don't think so. I've never laid eyes on him, but from what she told me I guess I wouldn't recognize him if I had."

"I can't think why he called me. We hadn't had any contact since he threw a blanket over that shooting downtown, the one that made Catherine a widow. I haven't thought about him in years; he wasn't worth the waste of brain cells. I don't get on with killers, even when they carry a license."

"I'm still working on how he found out about her. This service is invitation only. She made out the list. I never met half these people before today. Assuming you were right about his connections, doesn't the CIA have a mandatory retirement policy?"

"They don't confide in me. My guess is they let you go when they don't need you anymore. One way or the other."

A thick vein pulsed on his forehead; until then I didn't think anything would shake him short of an explosion in a construction elevator. "Do you mean to say they still work that way in the twenty-first century?"

"No. They're probably more efficient about it now: Deadly sonic waves through a cell phone, maybe, or an exploding vape. When someone invents a better tank, someone else starts a war."

We were interrupted by some people who came to shake his hand and purr sympathy. I smelled perfume with names I couldn't pronounce and aftershave that didn't come in a bottle with a Viking on the label. He steered the last one away with an elegant hand on a linen sleeve. The well-bred smile was gone when he turned back to me.

"If he does turn up, I don't want to deal with it. Can you?"

"Is that what you wanted to discuss?"

He started to say something, but just then a stout man in a clerical collar stepped up behind the podium and thumped a microphone with a finger. We joined the assembly taking seats in ten rows of folding wooden chairs facing front and the ghastly thing got going.

TWELVE

Funerals are for the living, they say. I can't think who they're talking about."

I looked at Prosper through the steam rising from a bowl of pasta. After the group broke up we'd walked down the business block to the Villa Firenze, an Italian restaurant specializing in Northern cuisine, and taken a glass-topped table on an iron frame on an open terrace. Before our waiter left us he adjusted our umbrella to keep the sun out of our eyes. Here on the far edge of the Eastern Time Zone, in summer you can read the fine print on a mortgage agreement outside at midnight. It was pleasantly warm.

I said, "I guess it's like getting a splinter pulled from your thumb. It's no fun while it's going on, but when it's done it's done."

"Maybe. Anyway, she wanted it this way. As I said, those were mostly strangers to me. She worked with some of them; she was a buyer for a clothing store chain, you know."

"No surprise. She could throw together a red-carpet outfit in ten minutes."

"She bought me this tie. I never put it on before today. Some of the other people there she met socially, without me along. We led separate lives in many ways."

We hadn't been exactly joined at the hip, either; but I didn't chime in. I'd learned long ago to let them talk, whether it was business or personal. Meanwhile the fettuccini was good and the Chianti anesthetized the pounding in my skull. The prices on the menu reflected the gears the restaurant had to grease to set up in that location; but Prosper wouldn't let me pay my share.

"They seemed to genuinely like her," I said. "I overheard some funny stories afterward."

"Any audience was her arena."

She hadn't changed. Still, he'd outlasted me by a decade. There'd been something there for sure.

"We were a mismatch," I said. "The bitterness went on long after it had to. That was on me. She caught me on a bad day and it hung on for years."

"She said the same thing; about not being right for each other, I mean. You were just back from war, with all I suppose that entails, and formal police work didn't suit you, which is why you didn't stay long enough to get your badge."

That had been more the department's decision than mine, but I didn't correct him. It was something that had happened a lifetime ago, to someone I didn't know very well.

"For what it's worth," he said, "she was happy when you left the force. She never wanted you to join in the first place. It wasn't snobbery, or a matter of expensive tastes. It was a dangerous time to be a policeman."

"It's worse now."

He twirled a strand of linguini around his fork. It was as thin as floss. "It took her years to get around to telling me that. You might remember she wasn't one to admit weakness."

I wished I'd known she had any. It would've been one thing we had in common. "It worked out in the end, seems like. You beat the odds."

"I can't tell you how many times I proposed. It was a conversation I was having all by myself. Two strikes, you know? Talk about odds! She knew her box scores."

"Strike Two made me look not so bad. I think that's when the thaw started."

A polished green Corvette chirped its tires behind a truck stopped for the light. The noise was sharp enough to turn heads. I drained my glass and gave up on ever finishing an Italian meal in a restaurant. Pasta breeds and multiplies in the bowl. "Old times," I said. "Nuts."

He kept busy with his fork and spoon, but he was looking at me, not his plate. His eyes were kind, faded gray from being left out in the weather, but there was steel behind them or he wouldn't have been any use on a job site. He shoved everything away and folded his arms on the table. With his coat off and sleeves turned back he showed the forearms of an ironmonger. "These last few months?"

He wanted me to say yes, I was listening. Instead I just listened.

The steel was all that was there. Any kindness had been an optical illusion. "You didn't have Catherine under surveillance, by any chance?"

Just then our waiter came to ask if we wanted anything else. We shook our heads and he took away our dishes.

I shook a cigarette out of the pack and fooled around with it. It's almost as bad a habit as lighting up, but my reading glasses were in my pocket and I had no excuse to take them out and wipe the lenses to barter for time.

"No," I said, "I didn't. I wasn't even sure she was still in the area, and anyway I'm not well enough off to haunt people just for fun. What's been going on?"

"She noticed it first. She asked me what I knew about it. Because of my work, you see; there's no reason to try to convince anyone the construction business doesn't brush up against some shady characters on a regular basis. We deal in explosives and concrete—that's pork and beans to a certain element—and then there are the unions. I've been interviewed by the FBI because of some of my associations, but I pride myself on my records and bookkeeping, and I've never come close to being accused of anything. Still—well, it's the nature of the beast. So when Catherine said she felt we were being watched, I didn't discount it."

"Did she bring this up before or after she was diagnosed?"

"After. I know what you're thinking. If it weren't for the trade I'm in, I might have attributed it to her illness. There's still a lot medical science doesn't know about cancer; hallucination hasn't been ruled out, and in any case the very randomness of it all—the unfairness, as Catherine put it, considering all the attention she paid to her health—would cause the most levelheaded person to question whether she's the victim of some kind of conspiracy.

"After some time, when no evidence showed up to confirm her suspicions, I started to think that's what it was after all, her imagination." He took in air, held it like smoke from a joint, and let it out. "Well, you know what they say about just when you think so-and-so. . . ."

I dropped the cigarette to my feet and ground it into the terracotta, just as if it had been burning, giving him time to go on; but he didn't go on. "What did you see?"

"A blue Buick. The same blue Buick, several times, on the way to Beaumont for her radiology and chemo treatments and on the way back. *Only* on those trips, when we were both in the car. Never any of the times I was alone running errands or off on business."

He watched me. Anything I'd seen of a gentle nature in that face was illusion. It was the face of a man who could drop an I-beam on a human head from forty stories up.

"Walker, it was Catherine they were interested in: The woman I loved, and who once loved you. They were following her to and from the hospital all the time she was dying."

THIRTEEN

When the waiter returned with the check, I asked for coffee, laying cash on the table to spare him the trouble of adjusting the bill. Prosper didn't want any. I waited until it came and we were alone again. Then: "Sure it was a blue Buick?"

"One of the newer models, yes. Why?"

"Just confirming details." Federal departments don't mix their fleets; that makes it harder to tell friend from foe. The outfit tailing Shane Sothern was driving gray Chryslers. I wondered how many agencies were butting into my life this season, and what made me worth the expense.

Or if they were feds at all. Abelia Hunt and Shane might have been separate situations, and neither of them had to have had anything to do with me or a wife I'd misplaced when they were still in Huggies. When it came to politics, Catherine thought liberal was an arts program and conservative a style of dress.

"Can you think of anything she was involved with that would draw that kind of attention?" I said.

"Nothing."

"Anything that might be construed as other than, oh, say, an attempt to overthrow the government?"

"Aside from the godawful things politicians' wives wear to presidential inaugurations? No."

Some other time in some other circumstances I'd have admired his snark; this wasn't it.

I asked him if he got the license number, but that was just one of the questions at the end of chapter one of the primer. He shook his head. "I only saw the car from the front, in the mirror."

"Do you think you were *meant* to see it?"

"Open tail, you mean." A bitter smile creased the lower half of his face. "Yes, I watch TV. Maybe; but I'm pretty observant, and she spotted it first. How important is that?"

"It means the difference between someone who knew what he was doing and a raw amateur. If it's the first, it would help us narrow the field: either cops or an independent professional or the little gray army you and I and the rest of the taxpayers keep in uniform."

"And if it's the second?"

"Let's hope it isn't. Professionals at least are predictable. They run on rails."

"How can we—I—find out which it is?"

He was good. I couldn't tell if the pronoun slip was genuine. I sipped from my mug. The coffee had been boiling longer than Vesuvius. "We may not have to. If you're right and she was the one Blue Buick is interested in, it stopped when she did."

Blood stained his bronze cheeks. His anger was palpable, and it was directed at me. Even then he didn't shout.

"We have to. Because it upset her at a time when she had more than enough to be upset about. Because no one has the right to interfere with the most personal thing a human being has to face. And because of me. I want to remember the woman I've spent my life with without a cloud getting in the way. Maybe mucking around in people's private lives has made you numb to their emotions, but I'm not dead inside."

I set the down the mug with both hands like fine china. "Call me the next time you see the car, or any car you see more often than you should. That would mean whoever it is hasn't found what he's looking for. If he stays put for any length of time it will be a mistake, because I'll nail him."

"What if I don't see anything?"

"I'll muck around until I do."

"That was uncalled for, what I said. I should know better, the people I'm forced to work with on occasion." He drew a checkbook in a silver leather case from an inside pocket. I held up a hand.

"I don't need anything. That's my gift to Catherine. If the expenses get the better of me we'll talk then."

We rose. I gave him a card with my cell number scribbled on the back and we shook hands. I asked if he needed a lift.

"I'm walking. We're—I'm local. The dot-commers have driven most of the older businesses out here to the suburbs. They call my block Little Detroit. Ever consider it?"

"Considered. Rejected. Most of my customers share the three-one-three area code. They'd think I'm putting on airs."

On the way back to my car I rubbed the scar on my scalp, a souvenir of my last exchange with the Iroquois Heights Police Department; but I try not to knock a place a person calls home. In any case I'd poked a bear in mourning for its mate, which is rotten enough manners for one day.

I made the trip back home without paying attention to the turns; I knew that route too well considering my history. I was more interested in searching the mirror for gray Chryslers, blue Buicks, and a ghost or two of my own invention.

Her voice was vivid, as when someone shouts your name in a dream; clearly enough to wake you up.

I wish you'd let me lay out your clothes, Amos. You're the only one in the office. Why wear a suit every day?

I didn't think there was anything to what Guy Prosper had told me. Otherwise I might have taken money up front; a job is a job, and no one can live on bittersweet recollections.

Catherine had never posed a threat to national security. She knew fashion and fabrics and which celebrity's clothing line was going to break records, but she didn't know Moscow from Muncie.

The world's full of blue Buicks; also grieving spouses. Prosper hadn't earned the right to chronic suspicion, any more than I was qualified to sustain a healthy relationship for more than a week. Catherine had traded up in the end.

I picked up the *News* on the way home, but none of the corpses that had turned up since yesterday belonged to Gray Chrysler No. 1, and there was nothing about it on the evening TV report. That brought no comfort. Detroiters don't go out of their way to discover dead bodies, but unless the stiff at Atlas Motors hadn't clued in his partner on where he was headed from the Oasis Café, there was no reason Gray Chrysler No. 2 hadn't gone straight there after we lost him. And if Gray Chrysler No. 1 played it that close to the vest with his partner, why?

And was that the reason he was killed?

And how long would it take for the cops to tow an abandoned vehicle in a moribund neighborhood to the impound, trace it to some bureau named from leftover tiles in Scrabble, and connect it to the murder victim when he finally showed up?

And what made it my business anyway?

Every day of every year, someone gets careless and pays the price. You read or hear about him all the time, and just because you never looked the party in the face you shake your head, turn the page or change the channel, and lose yourself in some other tragedy. I had as much right as the next guy to be apathetic.

Except for the complication of a kid with a muckraker complex and a stack of Founding Fathers in the office safe.

I thought I wanted a nightcap, but I couldn't make up my mind even about that. At length I returned the bottle to the cupboard above the sink and went to bed. Fell asleep thinking about face-in-the-crowd men in plain-paper-bag cars and didn't dream about them once. That was one for the shrinks.

How are you, Amos? You've gotten so gray. I know a hairdresser who can take off years.

 That's kind of you, Catherine. You're dead, by the way.

 What's that to do with looking younger?

 You've got me there. I thought I had a good argument at dead.

 Did you and Guy get along?

 I liked him. Your taste is improving. Was improving; sorry.

 Don't run yourself down, lover. You weren't Husband of the Year, but you weren't Ike Turner by a country mile. We had our moments.

 I meant your other ex.

 Oh, him. He took all the sting out of being a widow. That's a long time ago now. Anyway I wasn't asking what you thought of Guy. What about what he said?

 Dying is a surreal experience, and not just for the one who's dying. You can't always count on your perceptions.

 That sounded stilted, even in the dream.

 God knows you had your faults, but copping out wasn't one of them. Of course, we haven't been in touch for twenty years. Men rarely change for the better.

 We're not in touch now. You're dead.

 Don't change the subject. You blew him off, I bet.

 I can't build a house without nails.

 I was wrong, Amos. You haven't changed. I'm dead, and you still manage to disappoint me.

I had a good argument for that, but just then I woke up. Something was different.

 When you've lived by yourself long enough, you recognize all the little breaks in the silence without having to think about them: the whimper of a doorframe shrinking from the drop in humidity, the thump and whistle of the *Flintstones* refrigerator kicking in, the gnawing of an urbanized mouse in the dugout basement. All these things are so much a part of the personality of a place you hear them without hearing. This was different. It wasn't a noise, exactly; more a stirring in the air, as if a window or a door had opened, or just the certain knowledge, born of instinct, that I wasn't alone in the house.

In my work a bedside gun is mandatory. It was in my hand before my feet touched the floor. I stood listening, a statue in jockey shorts, armed to the gunnels. I heard only my own shallow breathing. Moonlight spilled through the crack I'd left in the door for the cross-draft.

I crept around the silver patch it made on the floor, trying not to cast a shadow, curled my fingers around the edge of the door, and pulled it toward me, slow as the tide.

An irregular shape spoiled the familiar silhouette of the old armchair in the living room. It was a natural choice. Everyone who comes to visit makes a beeline for its deep cushions and pontoon-shaped arms. It's supported the sprung muscles of cops, pimps, grifters, killers, confidential informants, tax auditors, tramps of both sexes, and on special occasions its owner.

He wasn't wearing sunglasses now, but there was enough streetlight coming through the window to recognize him. For a beat I thought I was still asleep, caught in one of those dreams inside a dream inside a dream, like a hall of mirrors or the Morton Salt girl or reruns of *Friends*. My finger tightened on the trigger.

Not enough to trip the hammer; even if I thought shooting him would make a difference. I was sure I'd left him lying dead on the floor of an abandoned garage more than twenty-four hours ago.

FOURTEEN

You can keep the gun where it is, if you like. It doesn't matter. I'm unarmed."

That broke the spell. Dead men might get up and walk—they'd been known to do some pretty remarkable things as late as the autopsy—but they never make polite conversation.

He reached up and snapped on the floor lamp by the chair. It didn't seem to matter to him that I might shoot out of sheer nerves.

He looked older than he had in the check-cashing place; but then I'd only glimpsed him for a second, and on the run at that. It was his partner who'd taken early and permanent retirement on the floor of Atlas Motors. This one had a few more years under his belt, and what passed for family resemblance was largely a matter of posture, dress, and barbering. He could pass for a grad student, maybe one who'd entered on the G.I. Bill after serving in the Middle East: slim, tan, and physically smooth, as if he'd been turned on a spindle. He even had the Ivy League drawl. It would come and go, of course, depending on the occasion. His eyes, like his hair, were of no particular color. They watched me with all the warmth of expression of holes in a punch card.

Either he hadn't changed clothes or his closet was a year-around affair of steel-gray leather, charcoal worsted, and semigloss black lace-ups from DSW. Maybe it was regulation uniform for whatever tentacle of the federal octopus he represented. It would save precious minutes in the selection.

I lowered the Chief's Special. It was heavy and the grip had grown greasy in my palm. "I'm going to slip into something less comfortable. Make yourself at home: toss the place. But try not to make the mess you left at Sothern's. It upsets the housekeeper."

"I don't know what you're talking about; but be my guest." He made an agreeable gesture with a well-kept hand. It didn't look like it had ever made the acquaintance of a garrote.

I put on the clothes I'd worn to the memorial service, minus jacket and tie. I left the bedroom door open, but I couldn't hear the familiar sounds of a search in progress. That hurt my pride; I'd been marginalized. I clipped the revolver in its holster to my belt in the hollow behind my right hip. When a man tells you he isn't packing he has a reason.

He was still sitting there when I came out. He watched as I scooped matches and a pack of Winstons from the drawer of the table by the chair. I was close enough to take him then, and he knew it, also that the risk was minimal. He'd come for a purpose and he'd get around to it without the melodrama.

I offered him the pack like a good host. He shook his head and I sat on the sofa facing him and stretched a cigarette between my fingers. I worked up a smile. "Since you followed me home, I get to keep you, but you need a name so I can call you for supper. Geronimo? Agent six-sixty-six? Bubba?"

"They said you were quick."

He reached inside his jacket and snapped open a maroon pebbled folder with brass corners. The photo was a good lightness, with a hint of humor about the mouth. The name was Bruce Mainbrother.

I nodded, and the folder vanished. "You're my first Bruce. Why NSA? I thought suicide bombers were more your speed."

"That's ATF. But we all trade off when necessary. That's what the terrorist organizations do, so we fight by the same rules."

"So I'm a terrorist. Whose head did I cut off? I forget."

"This season we're more interested in the instruments they use than the terrorists themselves. They'd never have gotten within an ocean of the World Trade Center without inside help: not traitors, exactly, just misguided individuals who read an article on civil disobedience and took it to heart."

He paused there, as if scouring his brain for a more coherent way of expressing himself. That was the handbook speaking. I was supposed to use the break in the conversation to fess up and atone for my indiscretions. It was a waste of time and we both knew it. He'd kept what training he needed and paid only lip service to the rest. He was the type to go rogue.

I put the cigarette away. My mouth was dry enough to grow cactus. "Politics," I said. "Every four years, the same old thing. I'd rather lose money betting on the Lions."

"Does that go for your friend Sothern?"

I smiled again. My lips felt like I'd had a shot of novocaine. "I don't know how he votes. I hear young people don't anymore."

"He's a bore, like most of the assignments I draw. I let him duck out now and then just to break the monotony."

"He got away from you," I said. "Admit it. Amateurs do that sometimes just by accident. It was plain curiosity that put you on our trail at the Oasis. You ran my plate and wondered how a working P.I. happened to get a craving for Middle Eastern cuisine at the very time you had the place staked out."

It was my turn to pause, so he could bring up the subject of his partner; but he moved on.

"Abelia Hunt has nothing to fear from us, Walker. All we want to do is keep sensitive information out of the wrong hands. I'm an underpaid civil servant, not the Gestapo. My agency has a standing arrangement with the U.S. Marshal's office; the Witness Protection

Program is such a good idea I wish we'd come up with it ourselves. That doesn't mean we can't improve upon it. Her government is in a position to offer her relocation, employment, a home, and more importantly a level of security most Americans only dream about."

"When you see her, tell her I said good luck."

"You disappoint me."

"You didn't catch me at my best. Come back when I've had a shower and a bucket of coffee."

He lifted his palms from the arms of the chair, let them fall. "Everyone is right about you. It's like discussing Aristotle with a chimpanzee."

B.A., definitely.

He got up, went to the door, grasped the knob. "I almost forgot. I'm sorry for your recent loss. You weren't the indifferent ex. You cared enough to attend the service."

I had a sudden impulse.

"Who's driving the blue Buick?"

He turned back with an actual expression on his face.

"I only ask because I'm modest," I said. "You must think I'm a desperate character or you wouldn't change cars on my account."

He said, "Our contract isn't with GM. I can't speak for the competition."

"Okay. Probably a bill collector."

"You know, you're not as clever as you think."

I gave him that, partially because it was true; but I'd gotten something in return. He was going to find out who was leasing Buicks this year.

"I did my good deed," he said then. "Gave you a chance to help your country. The man I work with is younger and less patient."

A minute after he left, a motor started up outside and tires squished on asphalt. I opened the door to make sure the street in front was empty. I'd double-checked the lock when I went to bed, but it was unlocked now. He'd know how to get around a dead bolt without causing damage. The NSA budget would cover a burglar's kit that wasn't on the market. The one I had came from the back of a comic book.

I filled a glass from the tap and drank it down in one steady draft, like Bromo. I couldn't remember feeling more parched.

It wasn't a reaction to the lukewarm threat; that variety of benign intimidation was more convincing when George Sanders used it in *Appointment in Berlin*. What bothered me was that the only time he'd mentioned his partner was at the end, to set me up for good cop, bad cop the next time we met. It might have been bait; he knew bad cop was dead and wanted to slicker me into blurting it out. It might have been a thousand other things, any one of them light years above my pay grade. Either he was playing the game on a level I could only guess at or he honestly didn't know his act had gone solo.

If Mainbrother *hadn't* found the body, it meant he didn't know where to look. That brief exchange I'd witnessed back at the Oasis had been strictly routine. Double-oh-Dead had had a lead, or a hunch, and had kept it to himself. He wouldn't be the first to hog the path to glory and pay the price.

His partner would be back. That car would turn up, and this time he'd come armed; maybe with an arrest warrant too, if his type bothered with such courtesies in the current climate. He hadn't dropped *terrorist* into the conversation just to break the ice. The word alone was enough to neutralize due process. As if he needed the excuse.

I glanced at my wrist, but I'd forgotten to put on my watch. The clock on the shelf insisted it was five after four. It seemed later; summer dawns are unpredictable to the laity. I didn't bother going back to bed. The bad dreams are the ones that pick up right where they left off; the good are gone the minute they slip the hook. I brewed coffee, scrambled some eggs, and burned the last of the bacon. The coffee tasted like something strained through a pair of overalls.

Afterward I steamed out the poisons in a scalding shower, only to break into a fresh sweat while I shaved. The radio was predicting a heat index in the nineties and the first Ozone Action Day of the year. I toweled off again and put on a silk sport shirt, gabardine slacks, and woven leather shoes, the lightest things in my closet.

My visitor had left a scent that was still there when I walked back out into the living room: something crisp, like fresh-pressed linen. I couldn't think in its presence. My fusty little office was made for that.

A bloodshot sun was just clearing the river, but the garage already smelled like the locker room at half-time. I opened all four windows and drove to work, passing the morning shift on its way to River Rouge.

FIFTEEN

My building was in sight when I changed my mind. I drove past and swung west toward Dearborn. I didn't pick up any gray Chryslers or blue Buicks in my rearview, but that didn't mean anything if the season had ended on open tails. You can never be sure if you've ducked a shadow you can't see, and in any case all my latest secrets were public property, so there was no reason to run up my client's expenses at the gas station.

I hadn't heard from him, but the landline at the Oasis Café was probably tapped and his cell monitored. I didn't want any fresh material entering the record; especially if Shane forgot himself and said something that would make us a guest of Washington. That could have been yet another explanation for Mainbrother's visit, to scare me into a stumble. If his people had come up with anything to apply real pressure, they'd have used it by now.

A light burned somewhere in the back of the beanery, making a glow in the fake desert beyond the palms around the watering-hole painted across the windows. That would be the staff firing up the range and taking the chairs down from the tables. The glow put a fanatic gleam in the eyes of the *trompe l'oeil* chef sweating over his spitted lamb. The light at that time of day gave the whole scene a barbaric look, as if the world had stopped turning at the height of the Ottoman Empire. Any minute now the horsemen would come charging over the dunes with Khyber rifles.

Breakfast was in the works. It would be sweet and sticky: A cloying aroma of stewed figs and dates and thick syrupy coffee drifted out of the ventilator. It was enough to make me forget I'd had breakfast.

It was still too early for customers. I shared the rustic parking lot with some of the same vehicles that had been present last time: transportation for the help. As I sat there getting the lay of the situation, a barrel-chested party in a knee-length apron came out the back door and hurled the steaming liquid contents of a steel kettle into an existing puddle beyond range of the rutted walkway. I caught a whiff of rancid grease and dish detergent; that laid my hunger to rest. He paused to stare at my car, but I was hunkered down, chin level with the bottom of the steering wheel, and anyway the sun was hitting the windshield. He pitched the unfamiliar vehicle into the file of not-my-business and went back inside. From the look of him, a redhead with a face like a boiled brisket, he'd never been closer to the Valley of the Kings than County Sligo.

I snapped what was left of my cigarette out the window, got out, stretched, peeled my shirt away from my back, and scaled the outside staircase to the second floor. There a railed platform ran past a pair of steel doors set fifteen feet apart. The far one was sealed with an iron padlock the size of a dinner plate. The other was blank except for a chrome-steel cylinder lock that looked as if it had been replaced recently. That was standard procedure between outgoing and incoming tenants in the metropolitan area, keys having a way of migrating along with the transients.

My knuckles made a tinny sound on the battered brown surface. It was early, so I turned and leaned on the railing to admire the rest of the sunrise while I waited for Shane to shake out. A thin sheet of dew rose from the ground, billowing slightly, like mosquito netting riding a zephyr. The air had that scorched-metal odor of a long hot spell amping up.

When that activity lost its charm I knocked again. After ten seconds I tried the knob. It turned without resistance.

That's never a good sign, in Detroit or anywhere else. The friendly little hamlet where nobody locks his door only exists in old sitcoms and news reports of a farmhouse massacre. I fisted the Chief's Special, shoved the door hard enough to slam against the wall on the other side, and swung around with it, the revolver at arm's length in both hands.

Mine was the only heartbeat in the room.

It was an efficiency apartment, the room of a young bachelor: unmade bed, clothes chucked about, dirty pots on a two-burner stove, dishes in the sink, a stained mug, a crust of toast and a bit of egg pasted to a plastic plate on a steel kitchen table that someone had rescued from a scrap heap. A square fan turned sluggishly on the sill of the only window. The sole decoration was a piece of do-it-yourself string art on one wall that collected dust bunnies with splendid success and had probably come with the place. In a doorless closet a Red Wings jersey sagged from a wire hanger.

The room was directly above the restaurant kitchen. The smell of lard heating up on the griddle was strong enough to stand on its own, mixed with the fug of too many unwashed tenants and too much unchanged linen.

I opened the squat refrigerator, then slammed the door against the assault from inside. He had to have inherited some of the leftovers; no one could build up a stench like that in the short time he'd been in residence.

But there was nothing wrong with the room, if you were in your twenties and didn't expect to stay long enough for your cable lease to run out. For me it was only a couple of rubber checks away from the place where I might wind up permanently.

An afterthought of a bathroom contained a white porcelain toilet, a corner sink, a steel mirror, a gray dinosaur of a water heater dripping with solder, and a shower you couldn't turn around in without concussing yourself on the nozzle. The seat was up on the toilet, a relic; it would roar like a jet engine when flushed.

There was something missing besides the occupant. Just what it was swam across my brain like a floater in the fluid of my eye, only to dart away when I tried to look at it directly.

The .38 was still out, forgotten. I holstered it.

No cell. The phone that had come with the apartment was beige, the pioneer push-button from the Woodstock era, with no redial. I picked up the receiver, listened to the dial tone, and put it back. These days you can't tell from the sound if anyone is listening in.

All of a sudden that floater came to a rest. It hovered in place, naked to the eye: what it was that had been teasing me.

I went back into the main room, picking up speed: I'd lost my way and the faster I moved the sooner I'd find it. The shirt in the closet hung from a lead pipe. I scraped the wire hanger all the way left, then all the way right. A box elder bug hung crucified on a corner cobweb, opening and closing its one free wing slowly and without hope. It had no time for me.

Shane's *Nutty Professor* jacket wasn't there, nor was it slung over any of the furniture or on the floor. That blazer was as much a part of him as his shaggy hair and glasses in blue plastic frames. I went back to the bathroom. There was no sign of the usual assortment of dental and shaving stuff.

There wasn't a week's change of clothes in the place. No suitcase or duffel either. That's what had thrown me. I'd been looking for something that was there, not for something that wasn't. He'd taken just as much as he needed. He wasn't coming back anytime soon, and probably not at all.

A sprung wicker wastebasket stood by the bathroom door. It hadn't looked any too inviting on the first pass, but I was grasping at feathers. I dumped it out on the floor, squatted, sorted through wads of used tissue, an empty toilet-paper roll, a gnawed stub of green pencil. I could rub its point across a scrap of blank notepaper, reconstruct the message written on the sheet he'd torn off, and break the investigation wide open. All I needed now was a scrap of blank notepaper. As a wastebasket it was a waste.

I got up and stood in the breeze from the window fan, admiring the view of the parking lot and the wreck of my private practice.

A. Walker Investigations specializes in missing persons: It says it right there on the web site. A. Walker was doing swell. He'd been on the case two days and had failed to find a clue to the person his client wanted him to find. Along the way he'd managed to lose the client too.

My work there was done. I took a last look around, just in case a juicy lead stood behind me holding its breath, then let myself out.

Nothing had changed in the lot, apart from the shrinking shade and the growing bitter-iron smell of ozone. There was nobody to take interest in me as I went down the stairs and got into my hot-house on wheels and pulled out. The few pedestrians I passed on the street looked like squeezed fruit.

There was no place to go but the office; where as it happened half my problem had resolved itself. Some days are like that. You wonder why you even bothered to punch in.

SIXTEEN

It was actually bearable inside my building, or at least less like a cannibal's stewpot. The place was built back when ventilation cured everything from tuberculosis to athlete's foot, with high ceilings and aluminum ducts a man could crawl through without bumping his head. The windows were functional and so was the Slav who mopped the linoleum in the foyer; but not at the moment.

He took a personal day once a week, when for one hour his 1940 Philco picked up the sixteen-watt station in Royal Oak that broadcast Tchaikovsky, Rimsky-Korsakov, and "Lara's Theme" from *Dr. Zhivago*. The door to his ground-floor apartment was open for the cross-draft, spilling a Siberian jam session out into the foyer. He'd be in there doing the saber-dance and swilling Smirnoff. My theory is he's as Russian as a Chicken McNugget.

I paused to enjoy the current of air, if not the concert, then went upstairs to my reception room. There, someone was waiting to be received.

She was perched on the upholstered bench, stiff as a visitor to the principal's office. She'd lost weight since her photo op in front of the federal building, and her wash-and-wear business suit hung on her, but worse could be expected of the fugitive life than missing a few meals.

She'd found an empty laundromat somewhere. It wouldn't throw off a trained observer; even one who'd developed a habit for misplacing clients and their companions. The medium-dark complexion, childlike forehead, turned-up nose, and obstinate chin had still appeared in the news from time to time, although not as often as her lawyer, who had a gift for the colorful sound bite. Abelia's hair was shorter now; she, or someone who hadn't worked in a salon longer than a day, had hacked it off at the earlobes. It didn't make her look at all boyish. Rumpled as she was, tired as she looked, and ready to jump up and run if I twitched a shoulder, she was pretty enough to brighten even that room.

I opened big. "Miss Hunt."

She sat with her hands on her thighs, palms down. They contracted, contributing a fresh set of creases to her slacks. "You know me."

"It's the job." I started to unlock the door to the office, then thought better of it and used the key to lock the one to the hallway. She'd have had her fill of interviews across desks. I drew the Mission oak chair around and sat facing her at a conversational angle. I'd never sat on it before, and I knew then why visitors always used the bench. I'd only added the chair to make people think they were catching me on a slow day.

She sat still a second longer, then relaxed her grip and breathed. At that distance I noticed the citrus scent she wore. Even on that short acquaintance it seemed wrong for her. One of the periodicals I kept fanned out on the coffee table was slightly askew. It was a fashion monthly with a goddess on the cover. My unimpeachable training told me she'd made use of a scratch-and-sniff cosmetic ad. Daily hygiene is the first casualty of life on the run, and browsing magazines isn't an option.

"You're Mr. Walker?" Her voice was deep; a surprise. According to the reports she was thirty, but in person she'd seemed younger until that moment. Timbre like that comes only with experience. But then she'd gotten plenty of that in short order.

I said, "Who told you about me, Shane Sothern?"

"Yes. It was when he visited the first time to bring me some things. He said he was thinking of consulting you. I begged him not to. Just trusting *him* took everything I had, and that turned out to be a mistake. You don't know what I've been through."

"You're not the only one who's had to run from the law."

"It's a first for me."

"When he dropped by the other night, did he tell you he'd talked to me after all? Is that why you ran away again?"

Inadvertently I'd leaned in close. Her whole body began to vibrate. She was about to bolt. I leaned back.

Little by little she seemed to come down from her hysterical high. It was a remission, not a full recovery; but when she spoke again her tone was as low and steady as before. She was tailor-made for a job in an office where no one got very excited about anything. "You followed him from here."

It wasn't a question, so I didn't answer it. "He wanted to tell me everything, but something held him back; probably he was already regretting the decision. My guess is he changed his mind again. That's why he went back to Atlas: to try to talk you into letting him hire me. I *could* tell you that's how I figured it at the time, that I'm that good a detective. Truth is I was curious. I *am* good at that. It's what keeps me in business, apart from the long hours and the lousy pay."

She looked down at her hands, which had clenched again. Those slacks would never be the same.

When she raised her head again she was looking at the framed movie poster across from her. It was just something to look at when she got tired of staring at her hands. "He didn't stay long.

Agreeing was the quickest way to get rid of him. I guess I was pretty convincing. He left; and then so did I."

"On foot?"

"Yes." A ghost of a shadow of a wisp of a smile came and went. "I'm a speed-walker. It's how I stay in shape. How I *stayed* in shape before—before all this. Everyone here thinks you need wheels to get around; that's one of the benefits of not leaving Detroit. You can make good time when you're used to walking, and of course I find shelter during the day. That's the other thing about this place: lots of empty buildings."

"Hard to meet quality folk there."

She faced me full on; I'd been mistaken about the smile. "There are more dangerous places. Busy ones with lots of light, with your picture everywhere."

The windowless room was getting close. I asked if she wanted a glass of water, and took the slight dip of her head as a nod. I got up, unlocked the door to the office, and filled a glass from the tap in the water closet. The face in the mirror above the sink would've set a grizzly in flight. I drank from the glass, dumped it out, rinsed it, and refilled it.

On the way back out I opened the window behind the desk and turned on the fan. She hadn't changed positions when I brought her the glass. I left the door standing open and cracked the one to the hallway to stir the air. I peeked out. The hallway was empty as far as the landing; no mad Russians or robots who knew Greek philosophy. The creaky old stairs would sound the alarm if they tried to invade.

All this took place somewhere Abelia Hunt wasn't. She'd swapped a federal holding cell for the one inside her head. Even the heat didn't seem to affect her until she drank from the glass: Something glistened then in the ragged tendril of hair curling in front of her left ear. It took the place of tears. She'd have used up all of those.

I took inventory. Her skin was ashen. It hadn't been exposed to the sun lately, but I didn't need a medical degree to see that she was exhausted to the point of a nervous breakdown.

I cocked a hip up on the arm of the chair. It was a runner's starting position, but I was still at a disadvantage. Played out or not, she had youth and exercise and fear on her side. A deer will run for a mile with the top of its heart blown off.

"Has Shane made any contact with you since that night?"

"Of course not. How could he? He didn't know where I was."

"We won't get anywhere if I have to keep running bases."

"I'm sorry. I'll try to be patient, but—"

"Before you left the garage, did you see anyone hanging around?"

"Loitering? No. Foot traffic from time to time: Teenagers out past curfew, homeless men pushing shopping carts. One loud drunk who thought he was singing. Sometimes a car, but you've seen the neighborhood. It's not on the way to anywhere. I never saw even one police cruiser on patrol."

"You wouldn't, if you were looking for roof lights and the city seal. Cops don't advertise themselves in those areas; it stirs the pot. Not a gray Chrysler, pair of dark glasses wearing the man behind the wheel?" *A blue Buick,* I almost added; but there was no point in stoking her panic.

Her face went blank. She was thinking back, trying to picture something. Her head moved that same thirty-second of an inch, this time from side to side. "No. Do you know something I don't?"

I shook my head; lied. "A cliché. Feds think they're invisible in aviator glasses and a plain paper sack."

She decided to get mad. Her cheeks bloomed bright and her eyes—soft brown at first, circled dark as they were—turned gray as flint. "Now I'm supposed to look for something that can't be seen?"

I went on watching her. She didn't know anything about the

dead man in the garage. I may have butter fingers when it comes to hanging on to a client, but I know a little bit about character.

She was no enemy of the state. Persecution is hard enough when you're guilty without the added pressure of innocence betrayed.

I slid back down into the chair. I wouldn't be able to outrun her on a motor scooter.

"Why are you here, Miss Hunt?"

She answered right away. She'd been waiting for me to spit it out.

"Because you're a stranger. And just now, trusting someone I don't know seems less risky than trusting a friend."

SEVENTEEN

She was taking a chance with me, so I ponied up. We went into the office. That Grover Cleveland ventilation system conducted sound as well as air. I parked her in the customer's chair and cranked the fan up high. What it lacked in air circulation it made up for in volume.

The case called for extremes. Most of the business I conduct is confidential, but this one carried the possibility of listening devices in the age of *Star Wars* and Tom Clancy.

She'd said no to another glass of water. I leaned back in the swivel, open and friendly. "I can't make you a client. That would be playing origami with my conscience. I'm pledged to protect Shane, and trying to protect you too might mean throwing him to the wolves."

She opened her mouth, but I cut her off. "I don't want to know what state secrets you shoplifted from Uncle Sam. The more people you tell, the more trouble you make for them. You've already dragged Shane into your leaky boat. That's bad enough without me climbing in too."

"You call that conscience? I call it saving your own skin."

"I didn't say I was Jesus."

"Does trouble bother you, Mr. Walker?"

"It does if I can avoid it. The less I know about who on the Hill slept with a North Korean spy, the longer I stay out of jail. I can't run my shop from there. I'm not Al Capone either."

"Then I guess you asked the right question. Why am I here?"

"Because running my shop means pulling Shane out of the mess you both made, and you too if it can be done, without making a bigger mess in the pulling. So it's not so much a rescue as balancing a ball on my nose. Want the job? I don't, but it's why *I'm* here."

"I didn't ask him to help."

"You did when you accepted tissues and takeout when he brought them to the garage. That made him guilty of harboring. Anything he did after that, including hiring me, couldn't get him in any deeper.

"Don't make that face," I said. "You're two peas in a pod. All you had to do was keep your mouth shut and your head down and wait out your next performance review, just like all your co-workers. You chose to be Karen Silkwood instead. What made you do it?"

"I love my country."

"Not defensible in court. Try again."

I said it to keep her mad at me. Angry Abelia was an improvement on the martyr in the reception room. But she took the needle better than expected. She was quiet for a minute.

"I'm just a file clerk, a drudge too chained to the routine to open the folders and read what's inside. Classified material crossed my desk every day—sealed data assembled by people with top-level security clearance—and my job was to transfer it from the envelope to a drawer. I'd signed a non-disclosure agreement when I came to work, and that was supposed to make me harmless. Sterile. And all the time I was handling material that flew directly in the face of our country's principles." She laughed then, a short sharp bark; coming from her, it would startle a statue. "For a long time, I *was* that drudge: like the bank teller who handles all that cash and pretends it's Monopoly money. Then there comes the day when she puts it in her purse, goes out for lunch, and never comes back."

I said, "That's greed, not patriotism."

"Is it? Maybe she just got tired of her employers taking her loyalty and integrity for granted."

So it was a vanity issue; but I didn't raise it. She'd fly the coop for sure. With Shane somewhere out there in the bush I needed to keep the bird I had in hand.

"How does an entry-level clerical worker smuggle a top-secret file past FBI security?"

"Under my shirt."

I looked at her, flat as a plank. She brightened for the first time, glowed with something like childish glee.

"How'd I fool all those retinal scanners, motion detectors, lasers, and whatnot? That's the movies. The reality is just what you'd expect from government: ham-handed and sloppy. I think Washington loans technical experts to Hollywood and deposits the security allocations in the congressional slush fund."

"Now you're speculating. Stick with what you know and leave the rest to Oliver Stone."

She spread her hands. "Okay. I suppose you're right, but I had the material and I gave it to the media. They watered it down. They reported that private correspondence was being recorded, envelopes addressed and sent through the mail photographed and filed, but they left out—"

"They do," I broke in hastily, "all the time." She'd forgotten my speech about sharing details. "They're more concerned with ratings than assassination squads. PowerPoint presentations don't sell candy bars."

"I know. I knew it then. That's why I went to radio first; less slimy than TV, I thought. But they made a joke out of it. They ran it with the 'James Bond Theme' playing in the background."

She collapsed against the back of the chair like a broken kite. "I don't know why they bother trying to shut me up. Nobody's listening."

"The monkey in the middle."

"What?"

"Not important." I looked at the telephone on the desk, just to be looking at something that wasn't looking back. An idea was pre-heating in the oven. "I didn't wake up this morning and say to myself this is the day I throw over the government. But I'll see if I can keep you out of the file room in Club Fed without putting Shane there in your place. That's what he's paying me for, whether he admits it or not."

"I didn't ask him to. If I trusted my instincts I'd have stopped him somehow. I'm not asking any favors now. You wanted to know why I came here; I figured it out. It's because no one can think rationally when he's on the run. And now that I've had a chance to do that I'll be on my way." She started to get up.

"You won't make it to the corner."

"I've been outrunning people for weeks. I think I can outrun you."

"Stephen Hawking could outrun me. I'm talking about federal agents. The street's crawling with them."

Her hands were still braced on the arms of her chair, but she stayed seated.

"I've been made," I said. "That gray Chrysler I mentioned goes with a character named Mainbrother. He's with the NSA. He dropped by my house this morning. By now he's thrown a net over the block. That means he saw you go in, and he's waiting for you to come out so he can take you into custody without the trouble of snaring a warrant to enter this office. The neighborhood's too public."

The string that held her upright snapped. She bent forward and her whole body began to shake. The dry retching went on for a minute; then she put herself back together a brick at a time. It was worth watching, if only to store away for my own use.

"Maybe I don't care." She was as out of breath as if she'd run up two flights of stairs. "Maybe I should turn myself in and save myself a perp walk."

"If that's what you want, we have to find a way around the welcome wagon outside. After that, call your lawyer. I know she's worried about you; she's said so on all the major networks."

"She's not a publicity hound. She knows I'm the victim here, not national security."

"She's a Constitutional specialist. You need a criminal attorney. It's a murder beef now."

She stared.

"If it isn't," I said, "it will be when they find out. Mainbrother must be wondering what's happened to his twin." I told her about the dead man at Atlas.

She swung her head. "You're lying. You're trying to scare me."

"That's what I've been doing handstands to avoid. I didn't tell you before because I didn't want to send you stumbling into their trap."

She was sharper than most. She jumped from denial straight past acceptance to resignation in a heartbeat. She drew herself up and lifted her chin.

"What do you have in mind?"

"First we need to find a phone."

"What's the matter with yours?"

"You know what's the matter with it."

"Oh." She flushed. "Of course."

"They *better* have tapped my line," I said. "I'll be disappointed if they didn't. If I'm not a serious threat, what am I?"

"I know the feeling." She was eager now, hands on knees, ready to spring, but not away from me. "Who are we calling?"

"One thing at a time." I looked down at her feet. "Flats. Good."

"Why?"

"Heels and fire escapes don't mix."

Standing, I thought of something. I slid open a drawer and dropped my cell phone inside. "Yours, too," I said. "It's a direct line to D.C."

"They took it away when I was arrested. I called Shane on a pay phone when I needed anything."

"You're a better detective than I am if you found one."

I offered her a hand up. She took it. The magazine cologne had started to fade; I caught the scent of warm skin. All fugitives should smell so good.

The landline rang. It stopped by the time we got to the waiting room; then my cell went off in the drawer. It was probably either Shane Sothern, checking in finally, or Barry Stackpole to tell me it was the NSA I was dealing with: Our forty-eight hours had expired.

I didn't go back. From here on out, Abelia Hunt and I would leave the twenty-first century behind.

EIGHTEEN

The office three doors down from mine was rented that year, but it was just a drop site for a mail-order firm that bought the plates to government pamphlets, reprinted the material between gaudy covers, and sold them at $19.99 apiece plus shipping; the U.S. distributed them for free. It was strictly legal, but I'll take an honest thief any day. Somebody came around twice a month to collect the orders heaped under the mail slot.

This wasn't one of those days.

"Stay here," I told Abelia at the door. "If you see anyone, sing out."

"You wouldn't say that if you ever heard me sing."

I liked her. She was going to be trouble.

I slipped the latch with the strip of spring steel designed to reinforce my billfold, stepped over the sucker pile, and leaned on the windowsill to make sure the scrap hounds hadn't made off with the fire escape.

If it didn't come in handy just then, I wouldn't have missed that pile of iron. It had already seen one fatal shooting, part of another case I should have left alone. But then if I had a crystal ball I'd be out of a job.

It was still there, but it wasn't an escape.

A bundle of soiled laundry with a man standing inside it leaned on a Dumpster across the street, smoking a butt and waiting for someone to come out of the lunch wagon on the corner and dump yesterday's special. He's a permanence outside every hash house in town, fixed or on wheels. Only this wagon had been boarded up since *Seinfeld*; there wasn't a morsel left even for the rats. The sanitation services had forgotten the Dumpster was there. It was now the summer residence of the local derelict, which this character was not. For one thing, Grand River Charlie dressed better.

It's a rule of nature: For every Eliot Ness on the government payroll there's a Barney Fife.

But even Bruce Mainbrother had to take the men he was assigned; if he was in charge. He had point man written all over him. He'd be in a command post soon, if he didn't blow up first. And if he could manage to station all the duffers in right field where they did less harm.

I went back out in the hall, motioned to Abelia to stay put, and took the stairs down to the second floor.

The door stood open to the office directly below mine, for the cross-draft. This one had a receptionist. We passed each other sometimes, fellow travelers in the world of commerce who seldom had anything to say to each other. She worked for her brother.

She perked up when I entered, then saw who it was and slumped back into whatever game she was playing on her phone. She was a cute little brunette who belonged on a dashboard. The brother had hired her for window dressing. If he paid her to guard the gate, though, it wasn't enough. I walked right past her into the private office, looked around, and said, "Hello, Woody. Still no Oscar?"

The boy behind the Ikea desk looked less like Woody Allen than Woody Woodpecker. He combed and moussed his shock of red hair straight up into a pompadour and his nose hung so far out over his chin it cast a shadow. He didn't look up from the laptop on the desk. "Not yet. And the name's Duane. I make documentaries, not neurotic comedies."

His great-great-grandfather had sold honey wagons to German

farmers and his uncles made rocket fuel out of refined manure. They'd given him three years to fail, then come back and become vice president in charge of air fresheners.

I remembered all that about him, from a conversation with his sister on the stairs. Meanwhile his name had drifted away like wheat seed.

The laptop shared the workspace with a flesh-colored phone, nothing else. It came with an answering machine and buttons to accommodate four separate lines; three more than the building could supply.

I pointed at it. "That work?"

"What?" He looked up. His eyes followed my finger, as if that were the attraction. "Oh. Sure! I have to interview people sometimes, for research. I can't risk discussing details over a cell, or even a cordless. This business is a den of—"

I picked up the handset and punched three buttons.

"Nine-one-one. What's your emergency?"

I gave the flatline female voice the address and reported a prowler lurking behind the building. She asked my name. I looked at the boy behind the desk, but I'd forgotten his name for the second time.

"Ken Burns." I tacked on some convincing details about my stalker. "Please hurry. I think he's armed." I broke the circuit. "That should give me ten minutes." I dialed another number.

When my party came on, I gave him just as much as he needed. My documentarian—Duane, that was it—eavesdropped; but it was his office, his phone, and I supposed it was part of his work. The sister hovered in the doorway: This was better than Angry Birds.

And then I was gone. I'm still expecting to see something on cable access with Duane's byline.

I'd left the door open to the drop site upstairs. Abelia was still waiting there; I counted that as a vote of confidence. I winked and went back to the window on the fire escape. Emmett Kelly had finished his smoke and unzipped his hoodie to ventilate in the heat—carefully, so as not to expose the holster. There was a cabinet post in his future.

Six minutes after I'd called 911, a city cruiser squashed to a stop by the Dumpster. Two officers got out, hands on the butts of their sidearms, and started a conversation with Emmett.

He was too professional anyway to flash his credentials out there in the open. I'd counted on that.

Just when things were looking like an episode of *Cops,* a pair of concerned citizens came around the corner, moving casually, arms out from their sides. One of them was Bruce Mainbrother.

No ID folders came out, but after a brief exchange the tension disappeared. The officers recognized fellow members of the species even if the classification differed.

I collected Abelia and we made tracks: down the stairs, out the front door, and across the street to my car. The coffee klatch out back hadn't broken up, and at that hour of the afternoon there was no traffic, on wheels or on foot.

Pulling out, I studied all the vehicles parked nearby, but none stood out as the kind of car that was designed not to. They were learning their lesson. Uber and gypsy cabs are even less visible than gray Chryslers and blue Buicks.

It was a long drive, most of it on I-94. Gray stone became green grass, trees ganged up on billboards, buildings got scarcer, then turned into barns and farmhouses and feed stores. The thermometer dropped, or seemed to; the combined body heat of too many people packed as tight as Vienna sausages was less a matter of physics than perception.

I wasn't alone in thinking that. Ten miles short of Ypsilanti, Abelia wound up her window. I did the same, but left a crack.

Something about the country makes me want to stick my head out into the slipstream like a dog. We were silent most of the way. The quiet hung lightly, at least for me. I'd done more talking that day than I had in a week, and it was probably longer for her; but after a half hour she turned on the radio.

She charged through ads for hearing aids, memory enhancers, walk-in bathtubs; everyone seemed to know how old the car was. When she ran out of buttons, she cranked the needle right and left and got more of the same. She fell into a slouch. "No FM? Sirius? DVD player?"

"No; but on the other hand, no Dixie Chicks." I took over and found a station that wasn't all talk-shows. The woman announcer finished with the nation and turned to local news: A corpse had been found in a garage on the northwest side of Detroit.

NINETEEN

So it's true." She was speaking to the windshield. "I almost talked myself into thinking you made it up just to get me to go along."

"I started to doubt it myself. The longer you go without hearing anything, the more you think maybe you made a mistake. That's how the cops trick murderers into returning to the scene of the crime. In books, anyway."

"What took so long?"

"It shouldn't have, in hot weather."

"Do you think it was a cover-up? God! Do you—"

"It wouldn't be the first time. They're trained for it. Mainbrother's one cold son of a bitch. He'd strangle a brother spy and stop to tie his shoelaces on the way out."

"There are people like that?"

"I knew one."

We left the interstate, took a two-lane blacktop fifteen miles past farms and parks, and turned onto a side road that led to a lake. Our windows were down now. A breeze brought in the smell of fresh water and fuel oil; a log-sided marina advertised speedboats and Jet Skis for rent at summer rates. Neatly dredged canals ran out from the lake like spokes from a wheel, with houses built alongside. Tin-roofed shacks kept company with sprawling redwood lodges, wooden rowboats with cabin cruisers.

The canals had been introduced with the cabin cruisers in mind. The rowboats were there already, so nothing could be done about them, apart from raising taxes every year until the owners were forced to sell.

The forty-foot trailer was a sty in the eye of the lake owners' association. It had sat on cinder blocks since before the association existed. The owner had a lawyer almost as crusty as he was, whose retainer took the form of a week's fishing every summer. The tax bill was appealed and the appeals were upheld.

We got out. The heat of the sun coming off the water felt good on my stiff back. It's a whole different season outside the city.

A twelve-foot wooden skiff bobbed at the end of a frayed rope tied to the dock out back. A man pushing ninety knelt on the edge of the dock, hauling up another rope hand over hand. He was naked except for a canvas bucket hat, baggy shorts, and heavy duck gloves with gauntlets to the elbows. His hairy breasts lay on a sun-browned belly that hung over his waistband, but his biceps, brown also, were the size of melons.

Finally he swung something streaming water onto the weathered boards. It was a cage built of ten-gauge wire, hinged on one side. It opened in two halves when he manipulated the catch with one gloved hand. The other held a stout stick ten inches long.

A scaly head at the end of a snakelike neck lunged at that hand; but the stick got in the way. The wood cracked, split by a beak like a parrot's. Before the thing could spit out what was left of the stick, the man got hold of a tail—a prehistoric appendage with raised dorsal plates—and jerked it off its feet.

Abelia took in her breath with a hiss. I suppose I did too. The thing was as big around as a car tire, triple-clawed on all four feet, with a thick shell covered in green moss.

"What *is* it?"

The old man heard her. "City girl." He stood, holding the thing by its tail away from his body. It had dropped the stick but was still working to clear its jaws of splinters. "This your first snapping turtle? He's waited a hundred years to make your acquaintance."

"What do you do with it?"

"Eat him. Her," he corrected himself. "I snagged enough of these varmints to know an egg factory when I see one. Females make the best soup."

"I hope you don't expect me to eat that!"

"Don't know what you're missing." He was walking our way, swaying a little, partly from the weight of what he was carrying and partly because of his bowlegs. He looked like a carved Buddha propped on top of a Chippendale table.

"Abelia Hunt, Leif Dixon," I said. "You'll excuse him if he doesn't shake hands."

"Leif," he said, rhyming it with *life*; which was exactly how I'd pronounced it. "My grandpap came through Ellis Island from Skagastöl when he was ten; lied about his age. The blood of Eric the Red flows through these veins."

"Not to mention Thunderbird, Jim Beam, and Grey Goose," I said. "Sometimes all at once."

Only his lower teeth showed when he grinned. It was the habitual expression of a shark. He'd bailed out of the old Detroit Gang Squad over artistic differences.

Leif wasn't a bleeding heart; but nor was he a redneck. He disapproved of lawbreakers regardless of race, creed, or color, with one exception: Anyone who stole from, swindled, or otherwise annoyed the U.S. government was welcome under his roof.

Abelia said, "Thank you for taking me in."

"I ain't took you in yet. Walker never says much over the phone. I know the feds want you bad, but I don't know what for."

I said, "I'll feed you the rest inside." Sound travels across water.

He'd stuck a duckboard porch onto the trailer and filled it with tools and junk. He paused just long enough to hoist the turtle into a galvanized tub and strip off the gloves, then unlocked the door to the house and disarmed the burglar alarm inside.

At first glance there didn't seem to be much to protect. The main room was paneled in cedar, paved with linoleum, and sparsely furnished: mismatched sofa and chairs and a kitchen table that could be folded away to assemble an extra bed, neatly and with a great deal of effort.

That was the living arrangement. Dixon conducted his business from display cases filled with handguns and racks of rifles and thousand-dollar shotguns. He supplemented his pension as a licensed dealer in firearms, all of which at night went into a tall steel safe bolted to the floor.

He saw me taking inventory. "I got rid of the assault rifles. Don't care for the company they keep."

A newspaper clipping hung in a frame on one wall. There was a picture of Dixon's late wife, a round grandmotherly-looking woman holding a shotgun. Four columns described her encounter with a burglar who broke into the house to clear out the stock while Dixon was away. She unloaded both barrels into the ceiling and chased him into the lake. He was still standing up to his waist in water when the police came, and refused to come out until she'd been disarmed.

Our host left us, went into the bedroom, and came out with his bare feet in moccasins, tugging a knitted shirt down over his belly. He waved us toward the ratty sofa.

"This better be good. It's gonna mean washing twice as many dishes for who the hell knows how long."

He was a good listener. He sat in a Morris chair with his stubby hands in his lap, his ruddy slab of a face blank, until we finished.

"Atlas shut down?" he said then. "They at least put up a plaque?"

I said, "Can she stay if she washes dishes?"

He looked at Abelia. "See your hands."

She paused, then leaned forward and laid them in his. He turned them over, gave them a pat, and sat back. "You didn't kill anyone."

"You read fortunes now?" I said.

"You don't have to be the Hulk to use a garrote, but they slash the hell out of your hands."

"Maybe she wore gloves."

"Could. Didn't. I was a cop almost as long as I been selling guns. Not that I give a rat's ass if she did. The only good fed is a dead fed.

"This stuff you lifted"—he was still looking at her—"you put it where they won't turn it up?"

"There isn't any stuff. They took it all back when they arrested me."

He spread his hands; like most people who earn their living with them, his were more expressive than his face. "You see how I live. You think I'm gonna split the space with a damn liar? Find another hole you can crawl into."

I straightened away from the table. "You'd be okay with her killing a G-man, but not with lying? You're squarer than that."

"Hell with you both. I got a turtle to kill." He shot to his feet, making none of the noises you associate with an old man getting up from a chair, crossed the big room in three rolling strides, and banged the front door shut behind him.

An old-fashioned electric wall clock above the gas stove made sizzling noises between ticks while Abelia sat, still leaning forward, looking down at her hands as if to turn up the secret to reading them.

"He was always about half-rough," I said. "Living alone all these years hasn't taken any of the bark off. I should've warned you."

She said nothing. She hadn't heard a word I'd said. I listened to the clock fighting to get a few more seconds out of what it had left. It had probably come with the trailer and was almost as old as its owner.

I excused myself and went out onto the porch, where he was testing the edge of a hickory-handled axe with the ball of a thumb. "Just in time," he said. "I turn more of these mossbacks loose than I eat. It's a two-man job; better with three."

"I don't think Abelia's in the mood."

He frowned, smacking the handle into a palm. Then he rolled his shoulders and hung up the axe. "Getting soft in my old age, I guess. I'll put her back where I got her and snag her again when I'm her age."

"You're soft, all right. I could be Ivan the Terrible and still be good cop to your bad."

"She tell you?"

I shook my head.

He blew air. "Brother, it must be dynamite. They want it bad or they'd of took her out by now."

"Just like your turtle."

TWENTY

said, "Well, I found a fugitive every agency in Washington was looking for, and I did it in three days. Give me a minute while I pull the Pentagon Papers out of my ear."

Dixon showed his lower teeth. "Leave the girl to me."

"I've been with her all day. It's going to take more than turtle soup to open her up."

"The bar ain't so high. You found a missing person and lost your client."

He might work at that. Nobody's weak spot was a stranger to him.

I went back inside. Abelia was examining the arsenal in a display case. "Do you think he'd let me borrow one of these when I leave?"

"Do you know anything about guns?"

"About as much as I know about garrotes; but that won't stop them from charging me with murder. They won't bother to look at my hands."

"If they find you armed it'll just give them an excuse to save the country the embarrassment of a trial. Why leave at all? You couldn't be in better care."

"He's a mean old man."

"Dix? He can't even bring himself to kill that turtle."

She gave me a sad smile. "I need a few things."

She needed more than a few, but I wrote it all down, including sizes, and caught Dixon on his way back from the canal. I told him I'd be back pronto.

He figured it out. "I gave all of Esther's stuff to Goodwill or I'd save you the trip. I don't guess she had the same taste in clothes anyway."

The state road ran through a little village five miles away. I'd been there years ago. Not much had changed, apart from some new construction outside the limits. I bought a few outfits and some basic cosmetics and was happy to get out in under two hundred dollars; small towns will gouge you. The middle-aged women who waited on me thought I was Father of the Year.

Back at the lake, Abelia examined the merchandise with a polite expression.

"Next time call *Project Runway*," I said.

"It's fine. Thank you. I'll pay you back."

"That's on Shane. Assuming I find him."

"How do you know where to look?"

"I know where to start. If it works, I'll at least have gotten extra mileage out of an outlay I made the other day."

I asked Dixon if he had a landline I could use. He threw his chin at a beige rotary on the kitchen wall.

"Only kind I got. If the assholes want to listen in, they're gonna have to climb a pole. I can pick 'em off there with a lousy thirty-two."

I got out my book and dialed the newest number in it.

"Yes?"

That clear tenor again. He didn't sound any more cheerful than the last time.

"Mr. Rickey, this is Amos Walker. We spoke before."

"I remember. I'm not senile."

"Has Shane Sothern been in touch?"

Dixon's geriatric clock made noises like bacon frying in the little silence that followed.

"Did whoever sold you this number include the address?"

"Yes."

"I knock off work at six."

I listened to the dial tone, then pegged the receiver. "Dix, I owe you."

"Like hell you do, and you know why."

There was a bedroom at the end of the trailer. The door was open and Abelia was laying out her new wardrobe on the bed.

"I'll check back later," I said. "Don't go outside unless Dix says it's okay. Don't use the phone. This line may be clear, but any line you call won't be."

"Even my lawyer's?"

"She'd be the first they bugged."

She turned from the bed, went up on her toes, and kissed me on the cheek. I caught again that scent of clean warm skin.

The development in Farmington Hills was ripe with fresh sod and new money. Unlike Leif Dixon's sleepy little hamlet, it had gone through several makeovers just in the six months since I was there last: Roundabouts, ice cream shops, and shade trees had sprung up from nothing, and yesterday's corner lot was today's country estate. The cash flowed like tears on the Hallmark Channel.

A British ornithologist had lent his name to the sub-suburban layout, and all the streets were christened after birds, few of which were native to our climate or likely to endure it. There were flocks of ospreys, whip-poor-wills, and scarlet thrushes, all painted in silhouette on the signs. The one I wanted called itself Pelican Close, and came with the likeness of a seagull with a goiter.

I missed the place the first time. The address was stuck between a brace of flowering dogwoods, and in cursive to boot.
The blossoms had begun to lose their hold on the branches; every
breeze brought flurries of pinkish-white snow. The carriage lights
on all the corners sprang on just as I was getting out of the car,
but they were still on Eastern Standard Time: The sun wouldn't
be down for another hour.

I'd seen some of the movies based on Gerald Rickey's books,
but I'd never read him. His research required the cooperation of
convicts, ex-convicts, and people who would one day be convicted
of something. So did mine, and for almost the same reasons; but
that was work, and when I read it's to relax. But as I got ready to
ring his bell I wondered if I should have brought a book to sign.
Then again, he might hate that. I knew nothing about him beyond
the clipping Shane Sothern had shown me.

I rang the bell. I felt an eye staring at me through the peephole.
Then the door opened and the eye belonged to Shane.

They call them roundabouts for a reason.

TWENTY-ONE

You're a few minutes early, Mr. Walker. Jerry doesn't clock out till six."

I'd expected something more dramatic, God knows why. He had on his *Beautiful Mind* outfit: corduroy jacket, button-down oxford shirt, scraped jeans, and gray suede shoes, scuffed and greasy-looking at the toes; what the well-dressed academic wears to the student-faculty mixer in 1948.

"That's okay," I said. "I won't need him now."

What I did next was unscientific as hell; not at all the direction the seasoned observer of human behavior would choose to go. I snatched a double fistful of open-weave cotton, spun him around, and slammed him face-first into the brick wall next to the door. In the same movement I switched my grip to his right arm and cranked it up behind his back almost to his neck. Dogwood blossoms covered our shoulders like rice at a wedding.

I spoke through my teeth. "First the girl I'm supposed to save from the wolves vanishes, then the boy who hired me to do it. I'd rather herd cats."

"You don't understand."

He said something like that, anyway. He was talking to the bricks.

"I'm not supposed to have to understand. You're not renting my brains to figure out why you do what you do."

He sneezed into the wall; of course he had allergies. It was a release for us both. I laughed and let go.

We had a witness: a thickset woman in a tennis visor and a sundress printed with flags of the world. She stopped walking her toy poodle to stare. I gave her a grin and a wave. She tossed up her chin and jerked the leash. The dog was as outraged as she was; he'd been lifting a leg at one of the ornamental stones that lined Rickey's walkway.

Inside the house, someone was giving a typewriter the works. A chime rang and the typing stopped. I looked at my watch. Six o'clock on the nose.

"In or out, but shut the damn door. I'm not paying to air-condition the town." It was the voice from the phone.

I got a gentler grip on Shane's arm, steered him inside, and kicked the door shut with my heel.

The house was larger than it looked from outside; no Swiss chalet, but more than enough to accommodate a septuagenarian writer who'd buried one wife and was in the process of divorcing another, if that clipping hadn't lied. The room was open all the way to a pair of French doors with a flagged terrace on the other side.

In front of them a man sat with his back to us, drumming pages on a cherrywood table. He laid them down and swiveled away from his typewriter, an old eagle bald to the crown. His white fringe came down to the open neck of his shirt. It was a faded gray jersey with PROPERTY OF THE SOUTHERN MICHIGAN PENTITENTIARY AT JACKSON letterpressed on the front.

He swept off his readers and shut them with a click. His ears were each nearly half the size of his head; I figured that was part of the evolutionary process for writers. I felt his eyes as far as my hip pocket.

"Too spot-on," he said. "If I were to cast you as a private eye, the critics would say I slipped a notch."

"I get that a lot. Where's your secretary?"

"Home. *Her* home. She's not my mistress. Sorry to disappoint."

"Forgive the intrusion, Mr. Rickey. I'm having a hard time lately keeping track of my customers."

"You can turn him loose now. He's not going anywhere."

I gave Shane back his arm. I'd forgotten I was still holding it. He worked his shoulders, forcing circulation back into the bruised muscles.

Rickey said, "Have a seat. I may get a book out of this deal." He didn't sound retired.

"You won't want it. A lot of people with no sense of drama are already interested."

"So Shane tells me, but I'm too old to scare." He tapped his glasses against his palm. "What's your poison?"

"Anything but vodka. Ice if you have it."

He looked at Shane, who said, "Oh. Right away."

He half-sprinted through an open arch into a gleaming kitchen. While he was clinking around in there I found a chair and made use of it.

Rickey asked if I was married.

"Divorced; or I was. I don't know what I am now. She died last week."

"You're lucky. Mine's after the house."

I changed the subject. If he wanted to be a son of a bitch I wasn't going to feed him any more lines. "When did Shane come scratching at your door?"

He crossed one leg in sweats over the other and dangled a narrow foot in a carpet slipper. "Yesterday. I wouldn't have let him in except he waited for me to finish my nap before he rang the bell; he remembered my routine, and manners are scarce at his age. When I heard his story I invited him to stay: material's material. He spooked; who wouldn't, with all his life ahead of him? I'm guessing that corpse on the news is the one he told me about. Atlas hasn't changed."

"You know Atlas?"

"I had my brakes done there no charge, just for keeping my mouth shut: Suckers. Like I'd kill the golden goose. I changed the name of the joint and got three books out of it and one crummy film adaptation."

"I thought Shane did your research."

"He's hell in a library. Five minutes in a place like Atlas and they'd cut him to pieces with an acetylene torch."

"You're that tough?"

"I'm that old. What are they going to scare me with that a nursing home can't beat?"

Shane came back carrying a tall leaded-glass tumbler in each hand. Ice cubes floated in amber liquid. The young man drew up a chair and sat on the edge with his hands on his knees. He wanted a pencil and pad so bad it hurt.

I tasted my drink: Gentleman Jack, a bourbon I approved of. I told him so.

"Better and better. I don't stock vodka. People who drink it don't like drinking. They just want to get drunk."

I put the small talk to rest. "I'm not pitching a best-seller, Mr. Rickey. The feds know enough about Shane to know you're connected. That's dangerous."

He rolled his glass between his palms. "There are some advantages to being a recluse; especially an old one who sleeps light. I never leave the house long enough for anyone to bug it. I pay a secretary an absurd salary to transcribe my typed pages onto a computer. I've never been online. I'm too well-known to be off the grid entirely; but I'm a bitch to find."

"I was kidding about getting a book out of this," he said. "I don't want what you know. I've got ideas up the ass, more than I have life to put to use. I'm curious is all. Something tells me you are, too, only for different reasons. So let's drop the bullshit and cut to the chase. They say that on the Coast, honest to God, and I'm here to tell you without irony. But sometimes it makes sense."

"Okay," I said. "It's your house until your ex comes through that door with her lawyer. Just as a friendly warning, you might want to recharge your drink. This thing's like a virus, and if you think you're immune just because you're famous, you don't know your history."

"Son, I've got a file in D.C. as thick as your arm. I'm a Commie or a Fascist or a registered Republican; take your pick, it's there in black-and-white. I'll be dead before they finish processing the papers. I'm already immune on account of my age. My liver will get me before they even come close." He subsided deeper into his chair and opened his big ears.

I ran out of arguments.

I looked at Shane. "Who put you on to Abelia Hunt?"

I went on staring at him until he had no choice but to speak. "Why should I tell you?"

"No reason, except now he's killed a federal agent, why stop?"

TWENTY-TWO

The phone rang on the writing table. Rickey swiveled to read the caller ID, spun back. "My publicist. He wants to send me to Australia. I don't fly anymore. When I take off my shoes I want it to be my idea."

Shane waited while a New York voice honked out its message.

"He asked for me by name," he said. "This man. I don't know how he found out about me, or how he knew I was staying at the Y. No one knew that, not even Jerry. He asked if anyone was listening. He said not to respond except yes or no."

"Sure it was a he?" I said.

"That's the only thing I *am* sure of. He had some kind of speech impediment; slurred his words. More than once I had to ask him to repeat himself."

"I know the voice," I said.

He glared through his glasses. "If you know who it is, why are you asking me these questions?"

"Because you may have to answer them again in court, and you want to get your facts straight. You were talking to a killer."

Rickey said, "That's the second time you've said that. How sure are you he's your man?"

"I'm not, but I hope I'm right. Otherwise they're running in packs." I looked back at Shane. "'This man,' you said. Did he use a name?"

"Yes—I think. I was confused, and he was so hard to understand."

"He's slowing down. He's old; but it's the old tigers that massacre villages. Try to remember." I shut myself up. I wanted to prompt him, but putting words in his mouth would get me nowhere.

He looked like he was going to cry. He was making the effort to concentrate. It's a painful process with an audience present.

"It was something common, I think. That's why it's so hard to remember. Something with a *W*? Walter, Wilson—"

"William Wilson."

I'd blurted it. I couldn't help it.

"That was it! William Wilson. He *did* call you!"

"He used a different name."

"He should've stuck with it," Rickey said. "I could crap out a better alias. Nobody has imagination anymore."

"He has enough for his work. I know him as Frank Usher. That's what he was calling himself when we met, so he'd go back to avoid having to introduce himself all over again. He's used Edgar Pym. He has a Poe complex. It's the only thing gaudy about him."

Rickey smacked his thigh. "'William Wilson,' of course. A story about an evil doppelgänger. What kind of writer am I? I *have* slipped a notch."

Shane said, "It was a short message, for all the time it took to get it out. He said I'd find the woman I was looking for at Atlas Motors. He hung up before I could think what to say next."

"Who else knew you were working the Hunt story?" I said.

"Jerry was the first. I called him for advice."

I looked at Rickey. "Who'd you tell?"

"Not a damn soul. I don't talk about what *I'm* working on until it's finished. And he got no advice from me. I was still pissed he left me without a researcher. Can't believe he bought that retirement bullshit."

"Of course I'd been asking around," Shane said. "I had to start somewhere. I left messages at the federal building. No one called back. I called Janet Grasso's office, but the receptionist refused to put me through. I suppose I could give you a list: journalists, an ethics professor at Wayne State; let's see, his name's—"

"A buzz is a buzz," I said. "All it takes is one. Usher would have tracked you down if you only talked to your pillow."

"He found me. I guess it's no surprise he found Abelia."

"He's not so exclusive. I found her too."

He dragged his jaw up from his chest.

"When? How?"

"She found me, actually. I'm like Moses that way. She's safe. I dug a moat around her and stocked it with insurance salesmen."

The phone rang again. This time Rickey picked up. The voice on the other end sounded like a slow beat on a bass drum. I'd heard it before, and recently; but I couldn't make out the words and neither could Rickey, who asked to hear them again. He held the phone out to me. I stood up to take it.

"Walker."

"How was the service? I hope my flowers arrived."

Slow as he spoke, swallowed as were most of the words, the old sardonic tone ran through it like copper wire.

"How are they all?" My own voice sounded strange in my ears. "I didn't read the cards. What name did you sign?"

"I didn't. I wasn't sure how Prosper would take it. You of all people know I can be discreet."

"That's one word for it. Is there a point to this conversation, Frank? I'm kind of busy."

"Look out the window."

I knew which one he meant. It was the only one that faced the street. We had a straight shot at it from where we were. A blue Buick idled next to the curb. It would be the one that had been following

Catherine to and from her cancer treatments the last weeks of her life.

I closed my hand over the mouthpiece. "You wouldn't have a gun around this place."

"I wish you'd asked me that six weeks ago," Rickey said. "I had a honey of a collection until the settlement." His chair faced the window. "You know, this is one of the best-patrolled neighborhoods in the best-patrolled county in the state."

"They'd just make him mad." I uncovered the receiver. "Nice ride. How many bodies can you fit in the trunk?"

"Same old Walker. You weren't funny then."

"I'm not laughing now. What was it this time, a squabble across bureau lines? You spooks are worse than Ford and Ferrari."

"I'm retired."

"Hanging up," I said.

"Stay with me. A funeral makes a man take stock. I want to put the past in the past. I come with a peace offering. You've got questions, I've got answers. The ones you're getting from young Sothern won't do you any good."

"Answers first."

"Not over the wire," he said. "You know better than that. Let's go for a spin." He revved his engine.

I gave the receiver back to Rickey, who cradled it.

Shane had heard. "I'm going with you."

"You weren't invited."

"I'm the reason you're in this."

"The reason I'm in this is in the safe back at the office."

"Stay out of it," Rickey told Shane. "The grown-ups need to talk." He held his hand out to me. "Good luck. Wish I had that gun."

"It was just a thought. He's had plenty of chances to kill me before this." I shook the hand and went out.

The car was lozenge-shaped, the way they all are now. It was a model I hadn't seen before, maybe even an experimental design. You had to be pretty high up in the spy business to reach that pay grade.

"Mr. Walker."

I'd have known her even if I hadn't seen her all over TV for weeks, recognized her by her speech: that bourbon-and-butter accent that turns twelve-man juries into character witnesses for the defense. She leaned out from the back seat with the door open and a five-inch heel on the pavement.

"Ms. Grasso," I said. "The company you keep."

TWENTY-THREE

My attendance in Washington wasn't essential," Janet Grasso said. "Certainly it wasn't as important as reuniting with my client. So here I am." She slid to the other side of the seat and patted the upholstery next to her hip. I opened the door and sat down beside Abelia Hunt's attorney.

She caught me blowing on my palm. I'd burned it on the edge of the door; we weren't parked in the shade. "Here." She snapped open a shiny black handbag, shook something out of a plastic pony bottle onto a square of striped cloth, grabbed my wrist, and laved the palm with something cool and viscous. It drew away the sting on contact.

"Glycerine." She recapped the bottle and returned it and the linen to the purse; touched her cheek with a set of long slim fingers. "If more women carried it, they'd save a fortune on cosmetics."

It was a smooth cheek, artfully tanned. She wore her hair in a pageboy, cut along the corner of her jaw. Her nose just missed being classic, with a little dip below the bridge that brought up the tip. That bit of the perpetual child would keep her from showing her age at least until the glycerine stopped working. I tagged her around forty, but that may have been just the gravity of the impression she made. A well-toned thigh showed through a slit in her skirt.

Even sitting down she seemed tall. In the picture on the court-house steps, she'd stood a head above Abelia, but she'd worn similar stilts then and the girl barely cleared five foot two. Illusion was as much a part of a lawyer's tackle as a magician's.

The interior smelled like expensive luggage. Black, full-grain leather covered the seats and dash, a cockpit array of dials, gauges, screens, and speakers covered in black mesh. The windows were tinted solid black and the green glow of the dials was the only source of light. The air was Arctic cold. After thirty seconds I wanted a lap robe.

The car was a hybrid. It might have been running on ethyl or electricity or filtered sunlight for all the noise it made.

"How do you like it?"

The driver was looking back at me over his seat. He had the advantage. My eyes were still adjusting to the gloom.

"Swank," I said. "I always wondered what it was like to ride in the Batmobile."

"A gift from a grateful government. The lease runs out in September, but I expect mine will run out first.

"You're grayer," he said. "Put on some bulk, but apart from that you haven't changed."

He had, now that I could see; he'd become even more invisible. Nondescript late middle age had progressed to the level of decrepitude you overlooked on principle.

He was an old cripple, and even balder than I remembered. His dentures were too big for his mouth; he worried them constantly. The skin of his face, leaden gray, was melting into a puddle inside his collar. He'd poured his sagging flab into a purple velour jogging suit worn in spots to a greasy shine. He went with that car like a tramp in a four-star restaurant.

The steering column contained features that hadn't come from the factory: hand controls that took the place of foot pedals.

So that was what had happened to Frank Usher.

He saw me take it all in, and gave me more of his teeth. "My alibi, if you still think I'm responsible for that corpse. Cerebral thrombosis, commonly referred to as a stroke. It's been three years now. Took me nearly all of that just to recover my speech."

Which he hadn't entirely, and probably never would. It made for a delayed effect: I had to go back over his words to understand them. He kept a white handkerchief wadded up in one fist to blot up the spittle that streamed from the corner of his lip. That side of his face never moved.

I said, "I'd've sent you a get-well card, but I'd hoped you were dead."

Janet Grasso spoke. "You were right about him, Wilson. He's no politician."

"It *was* unkind," he said. "I was genuinely sorry when your ex-wife passed away."

"You were concerned enough to escort her to and from the hospital."

"That's one of the things I want to talk to you about."

"It can wait. I've been expecting you to drop around ever since you called. When I guessed you were Shane Sothern's anonymous informant I was sure of it. Now I see why it took you so long." I tilted my head toward the woman at my side. "What I *didn't* expect was that you'd show up with legal talent. It's out of character for a shadow warrior like you."

The half of his face that worked lifted, bringing with it the corner of his mouth. If it was supposed to be a smile it fizzled.

"Ms. Grasso is here as my guest. I asked her along in order to assure you that your interests and mine—and especially Abelia Hunt's—are the same."

Grasso adjusted the slit in her skirt, exposing more leg. Just because we're all enlightened now doesn't mean the old weapons are obsolete.

"You said you knew where Abelia is," she said. "I've gotten at least one such call a day since she left custody, but I know when someone's telling me the truth. It's my training."

"I didn't say I knew where she was. That would make me an accessory after the fact. I said I might have a line on her."

"You said enough. As Mr. Wilson"—she looked at the man in the front seat—"*is* it Wilson, by the way? It strikes me as conveniently generic."

"Usher will do. I haven't used it in years, but it saves confusion in this case."

"Not as much as you think." She returned her attention to me. "What have you done with my client?"

"That can wait too. Usher tailed my ex-wife all the time she was terminal. He was noticed; that was the point. Usher called me when she died, to make double-sure I'd connect with him in case Guy Prosper, her companion, didn't come to me to find out what was going on. Usher put Shane onto Abelia Hunt. He's obsessed with her for some reason."

I turned back to him. "There are too many spies in this story, and the fact that one of them at least is an experienced killer is too much coincidence, even if he can no longer swat a fly without help. Can your connections in Washington still be that good?"

I felt Grasso stiffen. I looked at her, at the slight change in her coloring. What I said had caught her up short. None of the questions I had to ask would bring any answers from that direction.

"I've been on the go all day," I said. "Missed the news. I thought they'd have identified him by now."

"Not yet," Usher said. "But his name was Albert Kreuzer, and he was a field agent with the NSA, on loan to Homeland Security along with his partner, Bruce Mainbrother; whom I believe you've met. Things were so much simpler when I was in harness. Back then all I had to worry about—aside from the enemy, of course— was not stepping on the FBI's toes. Now there are so many players on the field I'm not sure what game I'm watching."

He made a noise in his throat that didn't sound any more like a chuckle than his speech resembled human communication. It released a flood of spittle that he caught with his hanky.

"The CIA spent a couple of hundred thousand taxpayer dollars confirming my condition was genuine and—more important—that it didn't include dementia, and consequently an inconvenient lapse in discretion. No, Walker; I've no friends there when it comes to asking that kind of favor."

"Wouldn't it have been cheaper just to terminate you?"

"Under the last administration, maybe. This one prefers throwing money at a problem instead of ricin. And, no, I'm not your man. Whoever killed Kreuzer may not have had anything to do with Abelia Hunt."

Grasso took hold of the door handle on her side. "I think I need to absent myself from this conversation. We're drifting outside the bounds of lawyer-client confidence."

Usher kept his eyes on mine. "Go or stay, Counselor. You've served your purpose, which was to get Walker into this car."

She said nothing—and stayed put.

To me he said, "You asked why I went to all these lengths just to arrange this meeting. It was to put the investigation in your lap.

"I'm not the enemy," he said. "Not this time. Consider me your client."

TWENTY-FOUR

I need oxygen." Janet Grasso powered down her window. The smell of dogwood joined the canned air inside the car.

"I think we all do." Usher twisted his torso back around—the movement communicating his pain all the way to the back seat—and pressed the accelerator. We glided out into the driving lane.

I ran down my window. Literally in no time at all we were cruising a steady fifteen miles per hour along braided streets. As far as I could tell the development was laid out in the shape of an ampersand.

"I've got one client already," I said. "If this keeps up I'll have to install a second phone line. Just how many people are listening in on the one I have?"

"I didn't say I didn't have *any* friends, just none who will commit capital crimes on my behalf. IOUs are the life blood of the profession."

"That's not how you spell blackmail. Out of curiosity, what's the job? I should tell you my black bag's in the shop."

He glanced up into the rearview. "Counselor, we're heading into a gray area."

"Does it involve Abelia?"

"It does."

"I'll let you know if I get squeamish."

He drove with his head turned a little to one side. He had a dead left eye.

"Agent Mainbrother and his late partner were strictly fetch-and-carry," he said. "The NSA doesn't officially investigate homicide, but when the victim is one of theirs they handle it in-house and usually bungle the job because they're green. To save face they pin it on the handiest party. They've already tagged the Hunt woman with sedition and you can only execute someone once. They'll spring the trap under her feet and close the case."

Grasso said, "Pull over."

Usher put in next to a brick cathedral of a house with gables, mullioned windows, and a boxwood hedge that served as a security fence. I'd seen it in a documentary. It belonged to a hip-hop artist currently on an electronic tether.

She got out. "There's some shade in this block. Come back for me when I'm not about to be disbarred."

We left her in front of the house, fishing in her handbag.

"I studied law," Usher said, driving. "Back there is the reason I dropped out. They think if they stick their fingers in their ears and hum loud enough they won't get in trouble. The rules never change for them. Ours do all the time, yours and mine. Yesterday's friend is today's enemy, and vice versa."

"Watch your pronouns. I'm not one of you. I'm playing by the same rules I started with."

"You've never broken one."

"Not so you'd notice; as for instance the Sixth Commandment. I'm not a homicide expert either. Kreuzer was killed in Detroit, so the DPD should do the investigating. They're up to their neck in experience, and they don't have an axe to grind. Odds are they'll clear Abelia."

"You may be right; but they'll never get the chance."

A crew was putting the roof on a house under construction. Some of the workers had stripped off their T-shirts and tied them around their heads to keep sweat out of their eyes. None of them was older than my last oil change. You had to be young to work in that heat.

Usher drove well for a man with full use of only one arm. The motor made no more noise than a sewing machine as it wound through the sprawling tract.

"I've been a spy for more than sixty years," he said. "I've spent almost nothing of what I've earned since the Kennedy administration—hadn't the time—and now I never will. So I want to spend a significant portion of it on you. In return, I want you to clear Abelia Hunt and make sure nothing happens to her after you do."

In the dimness inside the car, dawn broke. I said, "You've been killing people in cold blood since before I was born. Suddenly you're a guardian angel, only with nobody to save, so you picked Abelia out of a hat. But you can't save her; you can't even climb stairs without help. So you reached into another hat and came up with me. I hired on to help Shane Sothern. It looks like I'll have to help Abelia too, because I can't do one without the other. Your clock's running out. You want me to make it a three-for-one deal and save your soul from hell. No soap. Save your money for a mausoleum."

"I don't blame you for doubting my motives."

"You're getting nobler by the minute. Take me back to Rickey's."

"I will, but first open the glove compartment."

I looked at it as if it was rigged to explode; but he wasn't going to blow us both up because I'd turned him down. He wasn't human enough have a vindictive side. I popped open the lid and looked at a multicolored sheaf of paper as thick as a leg of lamb. It was too many euros for the padded mailer to hold. I could barely shut the lid against the pressure.

"Quite the body count," I said.

"Do you know what the exchange rate was when the market closed today?"

"I told you I missed the news."

"At least take something for expenses. You're going up against Fort Knox."

"I can't afford your kind of money."

"You must want something."

I shut my window. The air conditioner was having trouble keeping up.

"I know you told Shane where to find Abelia," I said. "I figured that out before we spoke on the phone. What I want to know is why she told you."

Janet Grasso was where we'd left her, touching up her face with powder from a compact too large to be anything but custom made. She snapped it shut, dropped it into her purse, and got into the back seat.

"Take me to my client."

"That's up to her," I said. "When I find her."

"How long are you planning to play this game?"

"I don't know. It's like baseball."

"She gave up her right to make decisions when she broke custody. As an officer of the court I'm required to present her. I'm negligent if I don't try. I can end this right now, call the police and have you arrested: they'll hold you first as a material witness, then for harboring and obstruction of justice."

"They'll need evidence. If I knew where she was and I took you to her they'd have it. But you won't make that call until you get what you want; then you'll turn me in for extra credit."

"You don't think much of lawyers."

"Not all lawyers. Just the desperate ones."

She unclasped her purse, but no phone came out. She handed me a card on heavy pebbled stock.

"Call or see me when you've got it all together. We'll put everything on record. You came forward in the interests of good citizenship and after you discussed things with my client she agreed to surrender herself voluntarily, in the presence of her attorney. Usher needn't be part of the record."

I looked his way. He was busy mopping his lips.

"This case is a lawyer's dream," Grasso said; "but only if I bring her in myself and in person, before the authorities beat me to it. Otherwise I'm the attorney who lost her client."

"I know the feeling." I held the card without looking at it. It felt like currency. "I'll consider the offer."

She looked at a gold watch with a man-size dial. "I'm late for tae kwon do," she told Usher. "Drop me off at my car."

I said, "I didn't think anyone still took that class."

"I don't take it. I teach it."

Our route went past Gerald Rickey's house, but I didn't ask to be let out. Usher and I had more things to discuss without a lawyer present. At the entrance to the development we pulled up behind a BMW painted pearl to match her compact. She got out, fishing a pair of yellow leather driving gloves out of her Swiss Army knife of a purse.

Usher made a U-turn and booted us up to twenty. "Don't tell me you bought any of that."

"I'd like to see her in action. I bet she kicks ass."

"You trust her?"

"I trust her taste in stationery." I put away her card. "Tell me the rest."

"We'll have to go around the block a couple of times."

"That's okay. This seat's got lumbar support."

It was more than a couple of times; but it was a story that took telling twice before I believed it, and one more to believe that I believed it.

TWENTY-FIVE

had my case, up to a point. Now I had to figure out what to do with the client.

The light spreading across Gerald Ricky's lot was copper-colored, the air heavy with the smell of stale laundry we get that time of year at day's end. Some kids home from summer school or the zoo were shooting hoops across the street and making enough noise to flush the birds off all the signs.

No one answered the bell, so I pushed aside a drooping dogwood branch and walked around to the back. Fresh-clipped grass clung to my shoes, pasted there by the gathering dew.

A low brick wall separated me from the terrace. "Permission to come aboard."

Rickey jumped in his seat, slopping out some of his drink. "Jesus Christ! What are you, peddling coronaries door-to-door now?"

"I used the bell."

He wrung out his shirttail. "I believe you. I stuffed cotton in the squawk box so it wouldn't reach out here. Quitting time's quitting time. Come on ahead, since you're here."

I dragged my trick leg over the wall and stood with my feet spread, hands in pockets. "You're kidding."

The writer was sitting in an Adirondack chair, jingling the ice cubes in what looked like the same glass. He wore an aloha shirt and khaki cargo shorts; wasted limbs were the uniform of the day. His feet were bare in flip-flops and a dopey straw hat with a green plastic insert shielded his eyes from the setting sun. But it was the swimming pool I was staring at. The water magnified the ceramic tiles lining the bottom, each a reproduction of one of Gerald Rickey's best-selling book covers.

"My soon-to-be-ex-wife's brainstorm," he said with a snarl. "Had it done while I was signing in Chicago. She picked all the ones I hated. That's when I knew she was trying to drive me out of the house."

"I wasn't talking about the tiles."

Shane Sothern was swimming the length of the pool, straight down the middle like an athlete in competition. In black trunks with a silver stripe he looked less like Jerry Lewis and more like Michael Phelps.

"Yeah. Turns out the kid's an Olympic savant. Got through college on a swim-team scholarship. World lost another Johnny Weissmuller when he decided to become a hack. I wasn't around then to talk him out of it."

"You writers never miss a chance to run down your business. Competition that stiff?"

"I'm shooting pool with Shakespeare; you tell me. I only said I was quitting to make the critics think they won. It'll be that much sweeter when I bring out the next book. They've been writing my epitaph for years. I've got the skin for it, but I'm old. Why would I encourage anyone who's still got lead in his pecker to put up with that?"

I was only half listening. Shane climbed out of the shallow end and dried himself with a towel the size of a bedsheet. His muscles were smooth and moved fluidly under polished skin.

He spotted me and loped our way, shrugging into a terry robe that was too tight for him and retrieving his glasses from a pocket. By the time he reached us he was back to what he'd been; on the outside, anyway. He came with more sides than a disco ball.

"How was it?" he said. "Did he tell you anything?"

"More than I expected, but not as much as I wanted. He brought a lawyer with him."

"Just how many lawyers are in on this?"

"Just one so far: Yours. It turned into a consultation. She wants Abelia to turn herself in."

"That's no surprise. Her career's in trouble. What did you tell her?"

"She did most of the talking, which is what attorneys do. I'm supposed to run it past her other client."

"It's a trick, to lead her straight to Abelia."

"You think?"

"Where was Wilson—Usher, whatever—while this was going on?"

"He was an interested observer. He says he wants Abelia off the hook. Everybody I run into wants something, and I'm supposed to deliver it."

Rickey made an ungentlemanly sound in his throat. We both shot him a look. He waved the hand holding his glass. "Swallowed wrong. Sorry."

"You didn't hear anything," I said.

"Heard; don't care. I have my own fiction to think about. I just got three new ideas while you were talking, and your little fugitive from justice wasn't one of 'em."

Shane was looking at me now. "Did you believe him? Usher?"

"He told you where Abelia was hiding. Based on the trash in the grease pit in the garage, someone had been bringing her food and supplies before you came along; it might as well have been him. Probably was. Keeping secrets isn't a group activity, and with all Washington looking for her she'd have been blown before now if any more were in on it. Also Usher gave me a good reason to buy his story, or at least rent it until a better one comes along."

"What's that?"

I shook my head. "Get dressed. We've got a road trip to make."

Rickey said, "Don't go on account of me."

"If that's an invitation, I'll take a rain check. It's a long drive and secrets don't keep long."

Shane stirred. "I'll get dressed."

He didn't ask where we were going. His stock was changing by the minute, though I couldn't say in which direction.

I kept thinking about that athlete's body under the academic jacket. Garroting a man doesn't depend so much on strength as leverage, coordination, and a certain amount of physical conditioning. Shane had all three.

It was growing dark; the tower lights slammed on just as we entered the interstate. Gnats, moths, and whole generations of mosquitoes spun into the high beams, smacking against the windshield and leaving Pollock patterns on the glass. The ticking noises they made as they gave up their little lives had my nerves leaping over fences. I put the radio on and got nothing but static. I switched it off and made conversation instead.

"Good news. If everything's everything, you'll have a scoop by tomorrow."

"Scoop?"

"An exclusive, sorry. I forgot I'm old. Grasso's going to swap the files Abelia's been sitting on for the promise of a lighter sentence. She didn't say that, but she will; it's in the playbook. You'll be the first journalist on the scene."

"That's good." His tone was hollow.

"I thought you'd be pleased."

"I'm glad to have it, don't get me wrong. It's just that I'm more worried about Abelia than I am about making good. Why are you trusting Frank Usher? He sounds like the villain in every spy movie ever made."

"He's worse because he's real. But I'm tabling him until I can talk to her. The longer this thing drags on the less chance she has. It's time to lance this boil. Hang on."

An exit sign warned there was no re-entry to West I-94. I hit the ramp, cutting off a panel truck. The driver disapproved. I tromped on the pedal, slewing right and left on the curve and grappling for control. Shane's head thumped against the window on his side.

"Stay alert." I turned onto the access road that ran parallel to the freeway. "Might be more of those before we're done."

He brought his hand away from his head and inspected it for gray matter. "I changed my mind. I'm going to work in a shoe store."

"Can that. The act's growing old."

He looked at me quickly with a hurt expression on his face. The kid never broke character.

The panel truck had continued on its way. I didn't see any lights behind us; but lights can be turned off. I turned off mine, coasted for a few hundred yards, then swung into a gravel drive and scraped to a halt. A haze of pulverized chat rose and settled on the hood.

The drive ended in front of a cyclone fence with a tin sign that read AUTHORIZED PERSONNEL ONLY. Behind it in the moonlight stood a square blockhouse that advertised itself as a cement plant. I killed the engine and we sat there listening to the crickets and cicadas and a distant dog barking in the same cadence for two solid minutes. In all that time no vehicles passed along the road. I started up again and backed out.

I made more detours along the way. They added a half hour to the drive, but by the time we got to the lake we were alone.

It was getting on toward ten. Lights showed in the windows of the trailer, attracting bats. A waning crescent sent rippling fingers along the canal. Clouds of blackflies vanished when I turned off my headlamps. A few lights glimmered on the far side of the lake, as remote as stars beyond the moon.

"What a lonely place," Shane said.

"Not as lonely as Atlas Motors. Here, people look out for their neighbors." I reached across him and retrieved the .38 from the hidden recess in the glove compartment. He watched me. I read his expression. "We don't count as neighbors." We got out.

I had a police spotlight mounted on the left front fender, a thousand-candlepower job that threw a beam a quarter mile. I'd left the motor running and aimed the shaft at the front door. The place seemed too lonely for my taste.

The lens burst with a pop, followed instantly by a sharp crack and the echo of the shot growling away across the lake. Smoke twisted from the dead fixture. The stink of spent powder was sharp in the clear air. I returned fire.

TWENTY-SIX

A row of decapitated bass lined the front of the trailer under the roof, dry and brown as parchment, big mouths agape. I caught the biggest one square on the snout. I didn't want to put holes in the old man's siding, or for that matter in the old man himself; I had a pretty good guess who was behind the rifle.

"You owe me, Dix!" I called out. "I just had that spot installed."

"Walker, that you?"

"Like I'd say no." I put the revolver in its belt clip and gave Shane the all-clear. He'd thrown himself to the ground after the first shot. He got up and I leaned in and cut the ignition. Silence swallowed us whole.

The lights in the trailer were out now. They came back on and silhouetted a figure I recognized, short and squat with a rifle cradled in the crook of one arm. Dixon twisted around to look up at the shattered fish head.

"White Boy Rick," he said. "I stalked that son of a bitch ten years. You couldn't shoot one of the others?"

"I went for the one I thought I could hit. What's the idea? Your guest all right?"

"I'm okay." Abelia Hunt's voice, inside the trailer.

"Blow your horn next time," the old man said. "Bushwhackers don't. That's how you know they're bushwhackers."

"I thought you'd recognize the car."

"Since Studebaker went bust I don't know a Cadillac from a riding mower. Shake a leg. I'm not running an indoor skeeter farm."

Shane looked around. The crickets had started back up; the only sign of activity in the area. "So much for the neighbors."

"It's raccoon country," I said. "It'd take more than two shots to stir them up."

The furnace was running. The lake air was cool, and even crusty ex-cops chilled easy. Shane was looking at Abelia, a drippy smile on his face. She smiled back, but no birds chirped on her end of the exchange. Her shields were up.

But hers was the freshest presence in the place. She was scrubbed and rosy, and wore one of the outfits I'd bought for her, an open-neck polyester shirt and jeans pre-ripped at the knee. I'd counted on those being still in fashion. I smelled shampoo.

Dixon caught my eye and walked toward the other end of the trailer. On the way he stopped to return the rifle to its rack. It was a late-model Savage with a composition stock and an infrared scope.

"Twenty-two?" I said. "That's what you grab when you're under siege?"

He pointed at both his eyes with forked fingers. If he didn't need glasses at his age he never would. "Some of us don't have to aim for the biggest fish."

He beckoned me with his head. I followed him into the bedroom and closed the door.

"That boy's smitten," he said.

"He's got hormones. Don't shoot him."

"I got no beef with young love. It's the timing I don't like. He'll trip over his dick just at the worst possible moment and get himself killed. I don't care so much about that, but he might get us killed too."

"What do you want me to do, turn the hose on him?"

"I want you to keep your eyes peeled for when he knocks you

down trying to throw himself between her and a bullet. The ass-holes will be looking for that."

He might do more; but that thought wasn't ripe yet.

"Eyes peeled," I said. "Make any progress on that smoking gun she's got stashed somewhere?"

"She don't crack easy. What are they weaning 'em with these days, clams?"

"You're probably just rusty."

He showed his bottom teeth in that shark's grin; scratched his nose and left the finger there as if he'd forgotten it. "Did I *say* she didn't crack?"

He leaned in he dropped his voice to a rumble. I listened, lean-ing away from the smell of fish and gunpowder solvent.

"Hell you say," I said. "I was right there."

I've spent more comfortable nights on stakeout than on Leif Dixon's old sofa. It pulled out into a single bed, but it came with a steel bar that caught me right across the kidneys and whoever slept on it last used roadkill for soap. Abelia got the bedroom, Shane the padded benches in the kitchen that assembled into a cot. Our host, who subsisted on short naps at odd hours, stretched out in the Morris recliner and snored like a tractor choking on a Ping-Pong ball. We'd retired—the men, anyway—in our clothes, removing only our shoes.

We shared the place with ghosts from deer camp. It was a fug of cedar and moth flakes, slept-in wool, bacon and beer and fried onions and chronic flatulence, with a stale-oil finish courtesy of whatever fuel the old man burned in the furnace.

Shane slept steadily, his breathing even. He'd rescued Maid Marian and was dreaming of a wedding in Westminster Abbey. Outside, insects sawed away at their mating rituals, a bullfrog gulped. The electric clock in the kitchen wheezed louder in the wee hours.

I came to with a jump, as if someone had slammed a door. Until then I didn't know I'd slept.

My revolver lay on the floor with the grip handy. I grabbed it on the way off the bed and waited for my eyes to catch up with the dark. Shane was dead to the world, sleeping the sleep of the ignorant. It had been no sudden noise that had startled me awake: It was its absence. The crickets had gone silent.

I looked over at the recliner. Dixon wasn't in it. When the old man stirred, he made all the racket of a cat stalking a chipmunk.

A single green eye glowed next to the front door. It was red when the burglar alarm was armed.

It was 2:48 by my watch. I turned the luminous face out of sight and crept forward in my socks.

The door hung open. A snail would have beaten me to it. I crossed the porch, into a squadron of mosquitoes.

At the end of Dixon's dock a lantern burned, smoking with mist from the slightly warmer temperature of the water colliding with the night air. Someone was standing between it and the house. His back was turned, but the rifle he held caught the moon in a silver stripe along its barrel. It was a figure from a Remington painting: The settler defending his home from renegade Indians.

"Dix."

I whispered; a shout wouldn't have swung him around any faster. The laser sight of the Savage burned a hole in my chest. I held my arm away from my body, dangling the .38 by its trigger guard from a finger.

"Jesus!" He lowered the rifle. "Whyn't you blow a whistle? I got a lot less heartbeats left than you."

I let the revolver fall to my waist. "I just shed a bunch. What woke you?"

"Same thing as you." He cocked his bullet head toward the empty air. "Crickets: They're like watchdogs, only backwards; they shut up when there's trouble instead of yammering. And you don't have to feed 'em."

"You stopped snoring, that's what woke me up. Crickets can't tell a noisy muskrat from Jack the Ripper."

"That, or another piece of walking scrotum after my guns; but I don't like the timing."

The crickets started in again, stitching up the silence. He listened, then swung the rifle parallel with his legs. "We can go back in."

I smacked a mosquito on the back of my neck. It squashed juicily. "One of us should stand watch."

"What for? We got the bugs."

The lake at dawn was spread marmalade, but the beauty was lost on me. The thoughts I took to bed were worse than the snoring inside and noisy nature outside. Shane lay quiet and nothing stirred in the bedroom. When I pried myself out of the bathroom, Dixon was cooking breakfast.

He'd dressed for the part, in a wife-beater undershirt and the same baggy shorts, slinging a spatula like a fencing foil. Four hours of sleep had made him a new man. I sipped black tarry coffee, watching him crack eggs and hating his guts. The eggs were perfect globes, an inch and a half across and almost transparent, with leathery membranes.

"Where'd those come from?" I said.

"Freezer."

"When will you tell your guests they weren't laid by chickens?"

"When they congratulate me on my kitchen skills."

"Still think we had visitors last night?"

"Don't insult my crickets. Hungry?"

"No; and I'm okay with turtle eggs." I drained my mug and set it down. "I'll check out the car."

"About time."

The sun had cleared the trees when I got back, wiping my hands on a rag. The kitchen table was back in service. Dixon's guests sat facing each other on the benches, Shane in shirtsleeves, Abelia barefoot in a shaggy robe that wrapped around her twice with the cuffs turned back. Dixon loaded their plates with scrambled eggs and Canadian bacon. The diners looked fresh and energetic. I wanted to tie them up in gunnysacks and toss them in the lake.

"These are the best eggs I've ever had," Shane said.

Dixon was busy scouring the skillet. "Secret's in the shell."

That cheered me enough to wish our late risers a good morning. I ditched the rag and went to the stove to refill my mug from the coffeepot. Dixon finished the skillet and stood it on the drainboard. "Tell them about last night?" I said.

"I didn't want to spoil their appetite. I don't get to entertain often. How's the car?"

"It looks clean, but I'm as high-tech as a potato clock. A tap screw in the chrome could be a homing device in disguise."

"I got an idea."

I listened until I got to the grounds in the bottom of my cup, then dumped them into the sink on top of the mess from the big frying pan. "You might've run that past me before I crawled under the chassis," I said.

TWENTY-SEVEN

D ixon's rowboat bumped hollowly against the piling, riding the wake left by a Jet Ski. It was freshly painted red and green, a Christmas combination. Winslow Homer had used it as a model.

Its oars were shipped, pegged into iron locks. They were backup for the one-horse Evinrude that showed when the canvas tarp came off. The old cop had pulled on a checked flannel shirt and a fisherman's cap with a long greasy bill. He'd sweated in his white deck shoes a couple of thousand times; his big toes had gnawed them nearly through. He had a Colt 380 semiautomatic clipped to the waistband of his shorts, the pocket model that looked like a toy and kicked like a kangaroo. He'd locked up the .22 rifle. That meant he expected any shooting to take place at close range. I'd taken the hint and checked the load in the Chief's Special; checked it twice like Santa.

None of this was lost on Shane. "We're going back to Detroit? Does Abelia have to come along?"

She colored. "Have to or not, I'm going."

"Gloria Steinem's right," I said. "She knows what we're looking for and we don't."

He blew out some breath he'd been saving. "I suppose three men are better than one."

"Check your arithmetic, son." Dixon was filling the outboard's

tank from a metal gasoline can. "I'm just the boat pilot. I got a
business to run."

"You agreed to look after her."

"What've I been doing for two days, and not making any
money doing it? Wipe your nose and step up."

"If you're scared—"

"Easy, Red Ryder. Beating the crap out of fresh punks aggra-
vates my gout."

Abelia stepped in.

"Mr. Dixon's done enough; you all have. I picked this fight. I'd
go alone if I could."

"*I'm* scared," I said. "Thank you all for asking. Let's shove off
before I change my mind."

Shane caught on then: Dixon wasn't just killing time with the
motor.

"We're traveling by boat? Where to?"

The old man took hold of the starter rope. "Public landing
on the other side. My truck's parked there. That way the fuckers
never know if I'm home."

"What's the matter with Walker's car?"

The motor started with a sputtering roar, ending discussion.

I turned to help Abelia into the skiff, but I'm not fast enough
for today's woman. She already had one foot over the side. Shane
followed, keeping his balance; he knew his way around water. I
clambered in last.

We took our seats on the wooden cross-planks as our pilot cast
off. He guided us just above idle with one hand on the tiller until
we were clear of the canal. There he opened throttle and steered
us into the wind.

We had the lake to ourselves most of the way across; the Jet Ski
was a fluke, and long gone. On weekends, speedboats and pontoon
parties turned the place into a Dogpatch Riviera, but it was a business day. A brace of ducks glided in for a water landing, realized

they weren't alone, ticked the surface, and took back to the air. A bass with a head nearly as big as White Boy Rick's came up to gulp at a fly with a mouth the size of a politician's. We were as far away from the city as we could get.

Dixon cut the motor and turned us over to the slight current leading toward shore, steering gently by a single oar first on one side, then the other, paddle-fashion. We drifted onto the beach with a slight scrape. He bounded out and we followed, less flashily.

The old cop stood with his hands on his hips, staring at an aluminum rowboat tied up at the dock. The oars were shipped and there were puddles of water on its deck.

"Well, wasn't a raccoon or a muskrat last night," he said. "Smog-suckers: can't row for shit. Splashed more water into the boat than they put behind 'em."

I looked around. It was county property with unlimited access to the lake. The only structure aside from the whitewashed dock was a portable toilet on loan from the Department of Natural Resources. A broad limestone-lined drive canted up to the state road. "So they parked here and hijacked the boat so we wouldn't hear them drive up."

Shane and Abelia joined us. He asked what we were talking about.

I said, "We had visitors last night; early this morning actually. They were shy. They left before we made contact."

Abelia drew air. "Do you think it was them? Why didn't they try to take me this morning?"

Shane and I spoke simultaneously:

"Neighbors."

Dixon nodded. "We're a community. Back in the city they could blast their way in and nobody'd stir a hair. My guess? They wanted to make sure it was us and not some kind of decoy; wait till we're in the open."

"You mean like now?" Shane said.

"You asked why we took the boat. They're expecting to follow a car."

"It's a pretty theory," I said. "Let's test it."

He led us up the slope. A camo-covered shape dozed under a weeping willow whose pregnant branches sagged nearly to the ground. The cover was streaked with tree sap and bird droppings. It was almost invisible. I helped him roll it off.

An old pickup squatted in the shade, with rounded fenders and a divided windshield. The sheet metal was all rust-colored primer and primer-colored rust. Teddy Roosevelt had sat in it, with Harry Truman on his lap. It wasn't just ancient; it was primordial.

I grinned. "You never disappoint. If it was this year's Ford I'd have fainted."

"Clean energy's jake with me. I like to breathe, same as the next fella. It's them black boxes I object to. The spooks can track you by satellite all the way to Timbuktu."

Shane said, "Will it even make it to the main road?"

"She'll get you there, don't you worry. Tires are new and there's ten thousand miles left on the engine and transmission. Tank's full." He turned to me. "You want to pump the brakes a couple times, and leave plenty of room to stop. Replacements are scarce as pork chops in Jerusalem."

He was still looking at me. I knew what he wanted. I handed him the keys to the Cutlass.

"I'll treat 'em to the grand tour," he said. "Toronto, maybe. You can't get good Canadian bacon here in the States."

I pointed an elbow at the pistol on his waistband. "Try not to get any blood on the upholstery. I just had it detailed."

"Truck key's in the ignition. Been stuck there since ninety-seven."

I held out my hand.

"Thanks, Dix. Anytime, anywhere."

"We still ain't even." He went easy on me. I could feel my fingers by the time he pushed off from shore.

The cab smelled like sunned burlap, not at all unpleasant. There were three gauges in the unpadded dash, but only one of them worked. The others were cracked and frozen. We made a snug fit, with Abelia in the middle and a hairy specimen on either side to protect her from splashes and assassination.

The floor stick worked as stiff as a wooden leg. The relic rode like a coal wagon; every part moved independently. It was a beast that breathed. I nudged it up to forty on the paved road. There the pistons smoothed out and the tires behaved like suction cups.

Shane leaned across Abelia and shouted above the roar of the exhaust.

"What did he mean back there, about your not being even?"

I pretended I didn't hear him.

Leif Dixon's dead now, so I can tell the story with no risk to anyone but myself. The crook his wife had bagged all those years ago was released on his own recognizance after the cops fished him out of the lake. The judge didn't believe him when he muttered that he'd "get square with the old hag." After he turned up dead in Dixon's front yard with holes in his chest and forehead, the same judge wanted to try the retired cop for premeditated murder.

I testified at the hearing: The unregistered .32 found in the victim's hand hadn't been planted after his death. Dixon had acted in defense of himself and his wife, on their own property. I saw the whole thing. He went free.

At the time of the shooting I was three counties away, chasing the runaway daughter of a city councilman. Dix is beyond reach now and so is his wife, who fired both shots. If the case comes up for review, I hope I draw a different judge.

TWENTY-EIGHT

I saw the red-and-blue strobes before I heard the siren, and even that was belated; between the rumble of the exhaust and the smoke trail of burning oil, we were in a cloister on wheels.

I took my foot off the gas pedal and coasted onto the shoulder, remembering to pump the brakes. We shuddered to a halt. The three of us were packed so tight I could feel their muscles tense up.

We'd been on the freeway only twenty minutes; but it was the weekend and in that old crate we were ripe for the picking. I unhooked the Smith & Wesson and reached across my passengers to the glove compartment. It opened at a blow from my fist. I swapped the gun for the registration and proof of insurance and shut the lid.

I had plenty of time for all that. These days the cops know the full history of a vehicle while the tires are still rolling, but they like the thumbscrew. While we were waiting, I smiled at Abelia and winked. It felt as natural as a putty nose.

Finally the doors opened on the blue-and-white and two state troopers got out, taking their time. They pinioned us between them, hands hovering near their gunbelts, Wyatt Earp–fashion. The one on my side was black, an oak plank in a uniform cut to his measure. I had the window cranked down and handed him the papers and my license.

"The truck belongs to a friend," I said. "That's his name on the registration. I have a permit to carry a firearm." I held that out too.

"Where's the weapon?" His voice was a basso. So was he, by his tone. My old wreck was messing up his nice clean highway.

I told him. He bent down to look inside the cab and I saw his face clearly for the first time. His broad square face was heavily creased; he was old for his rank. There was a story there: one or two demotions had interrupted the path to commander. Metallic gray eyes prowled the interior, objects and people.

He straightened after a year. "Okay, hang on."

He and his partner returned to the unit.

"You took a chance reporting that gun." Shane's voice was shallow.

"State law. They can smell a piece a block away."

Abelia said, "Are we *sure* they're policemen?"

I hadn't thought of that. I should have; I'd been having too much fun double-pumping pedals and shifting gears on my own schedule. I looked at the rearview. They were on their way back, moving with that cat's gait the academy doesn't teach, gun hands hovering. Neither was holding my license and registration. I didn't like that; they were breaking the routine. Right then I'd have traded a thumb for a citation. I avoided looking at my passengers; Shane might take it for a signal and go for the gun.

At the car, the senior partner reached inside his blouse and brought out my papers.

"Great set of wheels," he said. "My grandfather had one just like it."

"Almost everybody's did."

It rang sour, I wasn't sure why. His tongue bulged his cheek. Leave it to a Mexican jumping bean like me to turn around and hop right back into the skillet.

"Tell your friend to fix that muffler," he said, and left. His partner went with him.

The three of us broke a sweat at the same time.

The congestion increased as we passed under the concrete

latticework of the overpasses approaching the city limits. Our town's chief industry was rolling fat, and the shifts changed as often as the traffic lights downtown.

The crawl, and the constant throbbing of the engine, was taking its toll on all our nerves. Shane had a death grip on the leather ceiling strap on his side. Abelia sat as rigid as Emma Bovary, her eyes fixed on the road and the thickening cordon of cars around us. If I were sitting any straighter I'd be wearing the headliner for a hat.

I threw myself on the sword: spoke as casually as I could at near the top of my lungs.

"What relation is Frank Usher to you?"

"He's my godfather."

The leather strap almost came off in Shane's hand.

I said, "That's what he told me, but I wouldn't take his word if he told me how my name is spelled."

"I can't think why he'd lie about it," she said.

"If there's a reason, he'd have it. If it's on the level, it would explain why a career killer would go out of his way to protect you from his own employers. I need more."

"My mother killed herself when I was two years old, and my father put me in a foster home. I resented him for years, but I came to realize that single parenthood isn't for everyone, and he did help provide for my upbringing. He died fifteen years later, when I was in business school. He'd managed to keep up my tuition and he left me some money, but it wasn't enough to support me and my education both. All I had in the way of work was an unpaid internship in the federal building downtown. I'd have to quit school and take a salaried job.

"Then I got an e-mail at home directing me to go to a room in Henry Ford Hospital in Dearborn. I was told nothing else, but since the message came using the private coded line I was assigned at the office, I knew it was important."

Shane had recovered. In the cramped space we shared, his glasses were superfluous. He snatched them off and watched her, his blue-enamel eyes looking indecently naked without them.

The girl had found her level, or maybe it was the story she told that made raising her voice unnecessary. We didn't lose a word.

To begin with, the number of the hospital room in Henry Ford she'd been given didn't exist. The woman who greeted her at the information desk lobby kept shaking her head until someone from administration showed up, looked at Abelia's ID, and asked her to accompany him; it was obvious the entire exchange had been observed by way of a security camera.

He worked a key in an elevator that took them to the top floor, used an ID card to swipe their way past a pair of sliding glass doors, and left her in a large room, bare but for a bed, a chair, and electronic equipment. A patient sat propped up against the pillows with wires connecting him to a bank of monitors that bleeped and glowed all through their conversation. He was an old man even then, and from her description we were talking about the same man. His speech was so slurred he had to add gestures to get her to supply a word or phrase he couldn't reach.

"He told me to call him Frank Usher—it was as good a name as any, he said—and that he was my godfather. I asked him why we'd never met. He said we had, but I was too little to remember, and that he'd stayed away all the years since; 'for reasons of delicacy' was how he put it."

The rest took patience on both sides. Abelia's mother had decided to take her own life after a lover had broken off their affair, and to make sure he got the message, to take her daughter with her.

"He said she bundled me up in a blanket, took me out to the car in the garage, and started the engine with me in her lap. A neighbor saw the smoke leaking from the garage door, which was closed, and called the police.

"'By the time they got there,' he told me, 'it was too late for your mother; but children are resilient. You survived. No one could shield you from the whispering at the funeral, but it's to your father's lasting credit that you never learned you were in that car. I don't think anyone could live a life unclouded if she knew her own mother had tried to kill her.'"

"'A life unclouded,'" I said; "he used those words?"

"Yes. He had a way of speaking—when he spoke, and wasn't using hand signals—that made it easy to remember."

He needed to expand his reading.

"The reason he said he'd decided to tell me all this is he wasn't sure he had much longer to live and now that I was grown I deserved the truth. He'd arranged to pay for my education and said that a salaried position at the federal building would be waiting after I graduated, if I decided to take it.

"He said he owed me all this as a man who'd abandoned his sacred responsibilities all these years, and asked me—begged me, I think it's fair to say—not to turn down the opportunity because of his neglect.

"I asked him how it was possible that he could offer me all that. 'You wouldn't know it to look at me now, child, but your godfather used to be somebody, and there are one or two people who haven't forgotten. Who can't afford to forget.'

"Mr. Walker, he smiled when he said that. It would have been grotesque even if he'd been able to do it with both sides of his mouth."

"I know the expression," I said.

Atlas Motors hadn't stopped deteriorating since our last visit.

Mosquitoes spun and floated above the roof, trying out their wings after their larval stage in the pond that had gathered where the timbers sagged. The whole building seemed to be imploding toward the center, with fresh cracks in the glazed tile siding. Wasps had started a nest under the rusted gutter. Police tape formed Xs across the empty doorframe and plywood panes, bright yellow against the smut; but official interest had vanished along with the corpse. We were alone as alone got in the middle of a metropolis.

Shane was quieter than usual; a Rapunzel with a murderer for a guardian didn't fit the image.

I pumped us to a stop. Steam gushed from the radiator; our horse was blowing at the end of the gallop. My passengers bounded to the ground. I joined them, not bounding. I cracked my spine and leaned back into the cab, smacked the heel of my palm against the lid of the glove compartment to pop it open. My revolver was gone.

TWENTY-NINE

Abelia and Shane were taking in their surroundings as if they hadn't seen them in years. I watched them through the discolored window on the opposite side of the cab. They looked as sinister as bunnies in a glade. You couldn't tell which of them was armed.

I reached between the cushions of the driver's seat, through a hole rotted in the upholstery, and fished something out from among the horsehair and batting. Leif Dixon's little Colt slid into my pocket as easily as it had into my palm when we shook hands.

Something stirred in the grass; what it was, we were better off not knowing. Some distance away a car alarm razzed and whooped for the better part of a desperate minute, then stopped, all hope gone. Apart from that the place might have been painted on a wall.

I swept tape aside from the doorway and we stepped into the clammy, unexpected chill of the emptiest of buildings on the hottest of days. I fingered the pistol in my pocket, watching the others, but neither gave any sign of doing the same. Abelia's fitted shirt and Shane's corduroy jacket both had tails long enough to conceal the .38.

Enough of the roof was missing now to filter in sunlight from above, a chiaroscuro effect although hardly artistic. The piles of takeout trash had settled into a kind of mulch. Scavengers had harvested the contents and moved on to other prospects.

An oblong clearing in the floor litter was nearly all that remained of Albert Kreuzer, another gray casualty in the inglorious war in the shadows; chalk outlines were going the way of the slide rule in a world of cell-phone cameras and holographic photography. There was a lingering odor that didn't belong to either stale kitchen grease or musty architectural decay. Frank Usher's favorite gothic poet would call it an evil smell, and he wouldn't be far wrong.

"Which one?" I said. The atmosphere called for hushed tones, but even those rang indecently loud.

Abelia put a hand to her chin, getting her bearings. Finally she pointed. "There."

It was one of the four steel sockets that belonged to the missing hydraulic lift. Like the others it overflowed with stained paper wrapping and shards of Styrofoam cup.

I took an eager step in that direction; stopped. I remembered that I wasn't the only one in the place with a weapon. I retreated two steps, creating a field of fire.

"Show me."

The look she gave me was bleak. Weeks on the run had put something in her, or more specifically taken something away. She would never again be what she was. She stepped up to the hollow tube, scooped out debris, and stuck a hand inside as far as the elbow. I looked for my gun; but I couldn't spend enough time on that and watch Shane too. I was one-third of a three-man standoff in a spaghetti western.

She rummaged for a week, breathing heavily. I was gripping the Colt so hard I can still feel the ache. Finally she gasped and hauled her arm up, all the way up from the bottom of the ocean with her fist closed around something.

I didn't know what to expect: blueprints laying out the plan for the invasion of Nebraska, the Pope's private diary, Colonel Sanders' eleven herbs and spices. Not the narrow cylinder that lay in her palm when she spread her fingers. It looked like a roll of Life Savers.

I showed my age. "Microfilm?"

"Flash drive." She bounced it on her palm. "Pages and pages of memos from one bureau to the next; not everything they've kept from us, but enough to change the guard in Washington if it gets out."

"Good. Put it back."

They were both staring at me.

"In there, it's a bargaining chip," I said. "On you, it's a death sentence."

I wasn't looking at them. They followed my line of sight to the empty doorway and beyond it the slanted concrete pad that led up from the street.

A car was turning in, moving fast enough to buck over the curbing: a four-door Chrysler, dishwater-gray with windows tinted jet-black. I'd seen it before, and also its mate from the same assembly line. It was still rocking on its springs when both front doors flew open. NSA agent Bruce Mainbrother piled out from behind the wheel; that was to be expected. Janet Grasso, Abelia Hunt's attorney and now Shane Sothern's, stepped out from the passenger's side; that wasn't. That's how it is when everything makes sense all at once.

THIRTY

How?" Abelia's voice was a whisper; the monster would go away if she just kept quiet. "Your car's back at the lake. They couldn't—"

"They could." I was whispering too. It was contagious. "I'm that dumb."

I took out my wallet and found Grasso's card. I turned it over, feeling its heft; it felt heavier now, but that was just tardy wisdom. I bent it double, dropped it to the floor, and used my heel to grind the microchip or whatever it was into the concrete. This late in the day, that accomplished nothing aside from emotional release.

Mainbrother and Grasso meanwhile had stopped a few yards short of the door. The bulbous pickup and unfamiliar plates had thrown them off.

The agent's hands were empty and the lawyer's were gripping her purse in front of her like a shield. I wondered about that handbag. People in showdowns don't usually worry about tissues and a comb.

I tickled the Colt in my pocket, but left it there. The tension was thick enough without sudden movement.

It was bright outside, dim inside, and from their angle they might not have been able to tell if they were covered. They were unsure of their next move.

I knew how they felt.

Grasso was key, that was clear; I just didn't know to which lock. Was she there as an NSA ally or a semi-neutral party? Accomplice or potential witness? If it was the last, Mainbrother was shackled. An unprovoked assault in full view of a civilian would embarrass Washington, and when that happened, Washington wouldn't look far for a scapegoat. He'd roped a wildcat and wasn't sure how to let go.

He stalled for time. "Walker?"

"Me. I'm haunting the place while your partner's out."

"Who's with you?"

"Come in and find out for yourself. Leave the ordnance behind. It's a gunsmoke-free zone."

"What makes you think I'm armed?"

"You weren't last time. I doubt it's a habit."

"I'll make you a bargain. You show me yours and I'll show you mine. Then we can throw them down together."

I looked at Grasso.

"What's your advice, Counselor? Or is that a conflict of interest? You can't represent Saint George and the dragon too."

She responded in her Kentucky cornpone. "You don't have a high opinion of yourself, do you?"

"I didn't say I was Saint George."

"I don't represent Agent Mainbrother. We happen to share the same interest: Justice for Abelia Hunt."

Abelia was standing behind me and a little to the side. She closed the distance, an automatic movement. It attracted attention from the two outside. I raised my voice to draw it back to me.

"That doesn't buy you a ride in a company car. Your business card did. It's state-of-the-art. You're only here because I slipped Mainbrother's leash and he wasn't in the mood to go back rowing on the lake." I watched her closely. "She's that important to you, isn't she? You said before she's a lawyer's dream; also a nightmare if you don't deliver her yourself after she gave you the slip."

She ignored that. Her face didn't. It went as white as a clenched knuckle.

She said, "You should be flattered. Those locator cards are custom-made. They cost a fortune. I don't have many and I don't like to waste them."

Mainbrother was impatient. "What about my offer, Walker?"

"I gave you time to think; now it's my turn. Who do you like for Kreuzer?"

"You just answered your own question. The identity of the deceased hasn't been announced. We towed his car ourselves and put it in a private garage we use sometimes."

"Harboring, obstruction of justice, and now murder. I'm a triple-threat. Except your outfit is leakier than cheesecloth. What else you got?"

"The agency wants to question Miss Hunt for sure," he said. "If you didn't kill a federal employee engaged in official business, maybe she knows who did."

"You'll have a hard time selling a jury a file clerk–turned–mad strangler."

He didn't get the chance to answer because all hell broke loose, as hell will.

I was watching everyone at once, and I saw the move out the tail of my eye. Shane was standing next to me, with me between him and Abelia. When he moved I chopped him on the wrist, a maneuver I hadn't used since the service.

It worked as well in civilian life. He gasped and his arm fell to his side, dead to the fingertips. I reached under the tail of his jacket and took back my .38.

Outside, things had changed.

Mainbrother was standing in a crouch with both arms extended and a slender blue semiautomatic in the standard double-grip, pointed at me. I was caught looking.

"Throw it out, Walker!"

I had no chance to aim. I'm no good with a hip shot; no one is. I couldn't go for the hideaway without attracting a bullet.

I gave the revolver an underhand toss through the door. It turned over once and kicked up shards of brittle paving when it hit the ground.

To Shane I said, "Kids shouldn't play with guns."

"Mr. Walker, I—"

"Save your breath. You didn't kill Kreuzer. Neither did Mainbrother. I worked it out finally: All three of us were on the way here at the time. You're still trying to impress the girl."

He turned bright red. I shouldn't have needed the jolt of memory to clear him of murder.

Mainbrother kicked the revolver off the edge of the concrete pad and lowered his pistol. "Come out where I can see you; all of you."

"First convince me you didn't bring backup," I said. "A squad of rooftop snipers and an armored personnel carrier."

"You're a hard man to bargain with, Walker, but I'll try. The main reason I brought Grasso along was to show her how we do things now. This isn't your father's NSA. We'd have found you sooner or later without the lawyer's help. You should know: We found that quaint hideaway on the lake."

"It's that royal *we* I don't like."

"Habit. We're trained to be team players."

"Kreuzer must've been out that day."

"So was Custer."

I made a choice. I hoped it was better than most of the ones I'd been making lately. I started for the door.

I was too slow.

Janet Grasso spun on a five-inch heel, dropping her purse, which was open. In that instant I saw that her hands weren't bare. She wore the yellow driving gloves I'd seen her put on before she got into her car back in Farmington Hills. Something swooped.

Mainbrother dropped his pistol to struggle with both hands against the thin supple cord closing around his throat. He was fit and in good health, but she had surprise on her side; also leverage, coordination, and a certain amount of physical conditioning. Tae kwon do wasn't as out-of-date as I'd thought.

Abelia started forward, but I moved in for a body-block, colliding with Shane, who'd had the same idea. The Colt was in my hand. I shoved him away and fired—from the hip. Black fabric fluttered under Grasso's left arm. Whether the flesh was punctured too was a question of inches; I wasn't close enough to see blood. She spun again, on the other heel now, let go of the garrote, and made a dive for Mainbrother's pistol.

This time I had a chance to aim. The bullet struck a spark off the barrel of the semiautomatic and sent it spinning out of her reach. She stumbled, one arm still reaching, caught herself, and straightened slowly to face me. The Churchill Downs face was gone; this one belonged to a treed leopard, more dangerous than ever. She showed no sign of bleeding or injury of any kind. That was all right with me. I had questions to ask.

THIRTY-ONE

Several dogs filed their complaint against our breach of the peace; they were good citizens, unlike their masters. For them, a little thing like a firefight didn't make a dent in the afternoon.

Mainbrother was even fitter than he looked. He'd unwound the cord from around his neck, slung it away, and stood, swaying a little, frozen in the face of the gun I had pointed in his general direction. He chugged air and his eyes were coming back into focus. He was flushed; his circulatory system hadn't wasted any time resupplying blood to his face and neck. The deep crease around his throat was dead white in contrast.

I was outside now. I backed them up with a gesture involving the Colt, bent, and scooped up my revolver from where it had come to rest. Then I went over and picked up his service piece. My bullet had messed up the bluing on the barrel without harming the mechanism.

Juggling them all was awkward. "Abelia."

She came out of the garage, accompanied by Shane. Both were staring at my captives. I pocketed Mainbrother's Glock Nine and offered her the Colt butt-first. "You asked for the loan back at Dixon's."

She swung her attention to it, shook her head.

I said, "I've got two people to make behave, and Shane blew his chance. Take the damn gun. Safety's off."

She took it. It didn't seem to mean anything to our captives that the angle of the barrel threatened only the ground at their feet. They didn't have anything to answer it.

Still, I felt naked and exposed out there in the open, and the choreography would be clumsy. I spoke to Shane. "Did I break your wrist?"

He grasped it with his other hand as if to test it. "No. Sore is all."

I took the Glock back out. "Don't make me sorry."

He took it.

I waggled the .38 the agent's way. "Be a gentleman and pick up the lady's purse."

He paused, then did as he was told. Janet Grasso watched him detachedly, as if it was someone else's handbag. The face she wore wouldn't win Miss Dixie.

I got everybody inside somehow. We spread out in a Stonehenge arrangement, three of us making a half-circle with the two unarmed parties facing it.

I held my free hand out to Mainbrother and wiggled the fingers. He tossed me the purse, still open.

I dumped it out on the floor, threw it aside, and sorted through the contents with a toe. Nothing unusual there except the oversize compact and a shiny blue smartphone with a heavy-duty screen protector.

Grasso had recovered some of her southern-aristocratic poise, standing with most of her weight on one leg and her hip cocked, disheveled but unbowed. She would stand like that while addressing the jury.

She spoke for the first time in a century. "You can't keep me here at gunpoint. I have rights."

"Everyone does," I said. "Killers especially. Where'd you learn how to swing a thuggee lariat? They don't teach that in martial arts."

No response. No one clams up quite like a lawyer.

"Doesn't matter," I said. "You can Google anything. The rest is practice and strength training. I should've figured it out when I saw those gloves the first time. I got distracted. Even mixed up my timetables. Everyone else had an alibi, not counting Abelia; but I couldn't make that one take. She was on the run from every kind of law, and yet she was the least desperate member of the cast."

Grasso said, "Go ahead, make your case. I'll shred it in court."

"Sure. You and Marcia Clark. Here I go.

"You ran into Agent Kreuzer right here in the garage, too late to catch Abelia. You weren't expecting him, but you put on your game face and let him search you for a weapon, including your purse, because of course you had nothing to hide. That scrap of fishline is thin enough to coil easily inside a compact the size of yours. He was looking for a gun or an edged weapon and wouldn't be likely to make the connection even if he saw it. You'd have an answer ready just in case he did. You won't find the mysteries of a woman's handbag in any manual."

Mainbrother was massaging his neck with one hand. The mark on it was changing color; soon it would put a gumball machine to shame. The noise he made clearing his throat made mine hurt. It sounded worse when he spoke.

"What did you hope to accomplish by killing me?"

She stood mute.

"Simple enough," I said. "After I threw out my gun, she saw you as the only threat, and acted from instinct. Probably she didn't plan to finish the job with the cord; strangling takes time, enough for the rest of us to recover ourselves and butt in. The play was to throw you off balance and get your gun; put a slug in you, then one in each of us, and plant the thong on your body: Just another federal agent who killed his partner and then everyone who might connect him to the crime. Pressures of the job and all that. Then Washington would bring in the cleaners and spin it however they liked in the media."

Grasso laughed; cackled was closer to it. "That's not just absurd! It's lunatic!"

"Sure. I was just spitballing. That ligature on Mainbrother's neck would be inconvenient; but when was the last homicide case where everything snapped together like Legos? You can't have everything. At worst, Kreuzer is just another open sore, like that mark around his partner's throat. They'll both heal. Meanwhile the Hunt file is closed and the confidential information she took back in lockup, or buried so deep it won't resurface this side of forever."

Mainbrother said, "We need that information."

"Not as much as we do."

"You're proposing a trade."

I was impressed.

"Your people don't know what they have in you," I said. "You're wasted where you are."

"State your terms."

"The government drops all charges against Abelia Hunt. Her arrest is stricken from the record and she's reinstated in her old job at the same salary and a fair recommendation when it comes up for review."

Abelia said, "I don't want my old job back. I'll find one that doesn't make me want to vomit every time I open a drawer."

Grasso said, "I want the credit for her exoneration."

We all stared at her; and by God, she didn't blush.

"I've earned it."

"It might do you some good at that," I said. "The overflow of public sympathy for Abelia could make the difference between life in the joint and lethal injection.

"You said it yourself back in Frank Usher's car: This case is a lawyer's dream."

"Oh, put away that gun. I don't need one myself. I have a brief-case."

Now I looked at Abelia. "Did you have Grasso's card on you the first time you came here?"

That sank in by degrees. "Oh, God. I found it in my pocket af-ter I left. I'd forgotten about it. I threw it away. I didn't think Janet would want any part of me after what I'd done."

I glanced down at Grasso's smartphone. It would have an app the manufacturers hadn't included: a direct line to her business cards. She was the original Girl from U.N.C.L.E.

A siren wailed, whooping at every intersection; the sound in-creased as it neared.

"What do you know?" I said. "Someone even in this neighbor-hood knows the number to nine-one-one."

I held out a hand to Shane, who surrendered the Glock. I gave it back to the agent.

"Your call," I said. "In a few minutes your fugitive will be city property. By the time your bosses work out jurisdiction with the locals, that hot coal you're after will be burning a hole straight through your career."

"How do I know it won't anyway?"

"Because as long as it's some place it can't be found, Abelia has a life insurance policy that won't expire."

"You've spent too much time in bad company, Walker. We don't work that way anymore."

"It wouldn't be the first mistake I made."

The sirens had entered our block. I had to raise my voice. "I shouldn't have to say that the same deal goes for Sothern—and me. We'd just muck up the plan you've already decided to agree to."

Scorn pierced the blank sheet of his face. "You want all this in writing?"

"It already is. But you'll never find it."

I should have seen it coming, but once you run into a string of blunders it's a hard habit to break.

Janet Grasso had stood still so long she'd seemed to accept the inevitable, was already planning her defense; it's how lawyers work. But all the time she'd been working her feet out of her high heels. And then she was sprinting, her long supple legs gobbling up yards at a stride.

Mainbrother threw himself into position, took aim.

The rest of us had a deep-lens view of the agent in his crouch, beyond it a woman running a diagonal across the asphalt lot, and beyond *that* a fleet of Detroit blue-and-whites squealing around the corner into the driveway, taking another piece off the curb. Then the shot, and the running figure throwing up its arms and hitting the ground in a pile of broken limbs.

THIRTY-TWO

The pickup seemed empty with just me in it. I stopped to fill the tank, buy bottled water for the radiator, and use the pay phone by the air compressor. Barry Stackpole didn't ask why I hadn't kept him up to speed; he'd spent months at a time off the grid, and for the same reasons.

The story I gave him was edited, but it was more than the authorities gave to the competition. I might have been the last person to call anyone from that phone. The next time my dark star brought me to the neighborhood it was gone.

Ten miles west of Detroit I drove into rain. Ten miles beyond that I crossed some kind of natural break in the atmosphere and suddenly the pavement was as dry as Aunt Martha's Christmas turkey. I wound down the window to blow the superheated air out of the truck.

At Leif Dixon's, all was as it had been. The old man was kneeling on the dock, hoisting his turtle trap out of the canal. He had on his uniform of cutoff shorts and nothing else.

I joined him just as he set the trap down on the deck. It was filled with cans of Pabst Blue Ribbon, beaded and glistening with moisture.

"Icebox is busted," he said. "I don't give a shit about the cold cuts and milk, but I sure as hell won't drink my beer piss-warm like a fucking limey."

Last time I was there I'd thought him the most profane man living. Now I knew he'd been holding back with a lady present.

I took charge of the trap, which was almost as heavy as when it held a snapper, and we went up to the house. We sat at the folding table in the kitchen and started opening cans. The place had that same masculine smell of gun oil and venison. Just forty miles away, everything had changed in less than an hour, but not at Dix's. Time there was frozen, like the gauges in his truck.

We drank two beers apiece while I brought him up to date. He was the first to hear the whole story and the last until now.

He belched Homerically.

"She must've been screwy. I never gave two shits for lawyers, but I always thought the bastards had more sense."

"Blind panic," I said. "They don't cover that on the LSATs. I was more on the nose than I thought when I was spinning whole thing out. Then the cops showed, right on top of it. When they come piling in like that it can drown out the inner voice of reason."

"Like I said."

I sipped beer, nodded. "She might not even have had to stand trial."

"You leave that little girl in jail?"

I flipped his key onto the table and slid his Colt across to him.

"The cops didn't want to give that back," I said, "or let go of her and Shane; but someone stepped in."

"Fed?"

"No. Abelia's back in her apartment and Shane's staying with Gerald Rickey, the writer, who'll probably offer him his old job; Rickey didn't stay retired any longer than Sinatra. I doubt even Washington will want to mess with a high-profile act like him. John Alderdyce said to tell you hello, by the way."

"He still a lieutenant?"

"There's talk of busting him down to deputy chief."

"Christ, I almost forgot." He took something from a shorts pocket and held it out. "It blocked the nozzle when I went to gas up your buggy; it was stuck just under the lip. Guess it was designed for a car made this century. Bitch to pry loose. Don't know what those folks in Tokyo are making their magnets out of these days, but it's as good as their electronics."

I turned it over in my fingers. It was a slick metal disc not much bigger than a dime but several times as thick.

"Mainbrother must've been fit to be tied when he figured out I left the car here," I said. "That tail Grasso pinned on me got her invited to the dance."

"What'd you do with the flash-whatsit?"

"Same thing I'm doing with this." I dropped the disc on the floor and smashed it flat with my heel. "While the cops were outside messing around I went back in, did what I had to do, and kicked the pieces into the grease pit. I couldn't risk them arresting me and emptying my pockets."

"You don't think Mainbrother will figure it out?"

"He will, when he has time to wonder why we went back. He and his team won't be looking for it in pieces; but they'll never stop looking. They're still searching for Jimmy Hoffa."

"So the stuff Abelia risked her hide for is gone for good. The spooks won."

"Yeah, but they'll never know."

He walked out with me to the Cutlass. He'd put sixty miles on the odometer throwing off unwanted company, but the fuel gauge read full. I shook his meat-chopper hand. "*Now* we're square."

"We're square when I say we're square."

He died of natural causes a week later.

THIRTY-THREE

never saw Abelia Hunt or Shane Sothern again. I don't know if
they saw each other, either. Love can be just a twenty-four-hour
bug, and she hadn't seemed all that interested.

The heat wave broke with a bang. My furnace kicked in around
midnight on the last day of June. It was going to be one of those
summers.

I got a call at the office. I picked up. "Mr. Rickey."

He hesitated. "Caller ID seems out of character for you."

"I got tired of hanging up on con games. To what do I owe this
pleasure?"

"I was wondering if I'll be seeing you at Leif Dixon's service.
You heard he died."

"You knew him?"

"From when he was still with the department. I didn't always
farm out my research."

"Who told you *I* knew him?"

"You did. You called me from his place. You're not the only
one who hangs up on con games."

"You know his number at the lake?"

"Who do you think bought my gun collection?" Ice collided
with glass on his end. "What about the service? Dress uniform
affair, mourning bands and an eighteen-gun salute."

"I'm gun-shy now. I tried to send flowers, but nobody sells thistles."

"Dix wasn't the crank he pretended to be." He paused again. "I know what you did for him."

"He told you?"

"He never told anyone. The first time you called me I was sure I remembered your name. I followed his hearing in the press. The rest wasn't hard to figure out."

"I can't think why you decided to farm out your research in the first place."

The cubes jingled again. He wasn't listening.

"I'll come clean," he said. "Dixon's send-off was just an excuse to get in touch. Are you working on anything at the moment?"

I got another call. The ID said it was from out of the area. I picked up anyway. A voice I didn't recognize gave me a room number in the Dearborn branch of Henry Ford Hospital and could I come over right away?

I didn't press for details. I'd been expecting the call for a week.

I didn't have to fight my way past the information desk. A tall well-tailored party who said he was with Administration met me in the lobby and keyed us to the top floor, where Frank Usher lay in a big corner room and left us alone.

The patient wasn't sitting up. He wouldn't, without help. He lay blinking at the ceiling, a wreck of human tissue with a face deflated on one side. A monitor beeped faintly; the bilious green line on the oscilloscope barely twitched. He was a mass of tubes and wires, and he gurgled when he breathed.

The eye that was still an eye crawled my way. There was recognition in it, but not much else. The hand that worked came up and clawed the oxygen mask from his face.

"I won't thank you for coming. You probably just wanted to make sure I wouldn't be leaving this room."

The second stroke had affected his speech further. It took him five times as long to say what he had to say as it takes to repeat it, and he hadn't the strength to signal for help when a word escaped his memory.

"Abelia Hunt's father was my target way back then," he said. "I started the affair with her mother to get close enough to do the job: my M.O., as you might remember. He was an operative, and professionally suspicious, but not of her. I spent almost three years laying the groundwork while the Company kept him on a desk where he couldn't do any more damage. But after she killed herself I wasn't going to make her daughter an orphan. I was already getting sick of the whole business. The brass put me on suspension for a year, but they finally figured out that both parents dying that close together would bring too much heat. They got him years later, but by then I was retired."

Three years. A professional of his standing could snare enough personal information in half that time to take down OPEC. But I didn't raise the point. Even a soulless assassin can fall in love.

He was still talking. "All that time ago I'd broken things off with his wife because she'd served her purpose. If I'd thought she'd do what she did—" He tried to shake his head; it looked like palsy. "Well, I was selfish enough to invest my nest egg in Abelia's future, to try to settle my conscience; and I was tickled pink when she turned whistleblower. That, I thought, bought me some time off Purgatory."

A spasm wracked his body and twisted his face like a wet rag. His lungs snatched for air; his lips were blue. I reached for the call button, but I didn't use it. His color changed and his breathing returned to what for him passed for normal.

"I've been a civilian too long," he said. I had to lean close to hear. "I should have seen Janet Grasso for what she was. It seems like no matter what I do, whatever my motives, I can't bring that poor little girl anything but misery."

The effort was too much. He closed his good eye and I thought he'd passed over. Then it opened again. He moved his mouth, but nothing came out.

I wet my lips. They were as dry as a cotton swab. I hadn't said a word for half an hour.

"Does Abelia know you're her real father?"

He tried to speak again and then he didn't. The monitor dipped steeply, then resumed tracking the barely discernible rhythm of his heart, but he was unresponsive, and after what seemed a decent stretch I left. I never found out if he was playing possum. The son of a bitch was a sphinx to the end.

Guy Prosper shook my hand and sat down at my table. The Villa Firenze terrace was the same ice-cream parlor arrangement of iron filigree and tempered glass, fenced off from Iroquois Heights' main street. The sun shining through our umbrella painted diagonal stripes across his square tan face. Today he was in work clothes: green twill shirt with flap pockets, carpenter jeans, and steel-toed boots. The outfit looked more natural on a general contractor than his funeral suit.

I said, "Do you drink? Catherine didn't cover that in her Christmas letters."

He looked at my glass. "Is that a Tom Collins?"

"Rob Roy."

"I'll have a Collins."

The waitress brought his drink and fled back inside; it was still chilly and she was in short sleeves. I'd had my life's portion of clammy garages, rustic mobile homes, and hospital rooms. I wanted to spend the rest of the year out of doors.

Especially not in hospital rooms; but I was glad I'd gone. For better or worse, the cripple at Henry Ford was the thing that bound us all together: my wife that was, the man she finally chose, and me.

I thanked him for coming.

"I had to," he said. "When I heard your name on the news I was sure it all had something to do with Catherine, but what they've been saying hasn't been helpful."

I left out the flash drive and some names that didn't matter, but gave him the rest. He reacted strongly only when I told him that Frank Usher had dogged Catherine all through her medical treatments just to draw me into the Hunt case.

"The son of a bitch."

"With apologies to bitches. All those victims, and the only one he cared about did it to herself. Like any man who comes to it late, he thought he had the corner on love. You and Catherine were just means to his motive."

He finished his Collins and signaled for seconds. "This was good of you, Amos. It puts an end to the business."

"What will you do now?"

"I haven't had time to think. That's what funerals are for, to occupy your thoughts. What about you? I know about relationships. When they end they don't always end."

"Work," I said. "A big-time writer offered me a divorce job. It might even put me in a tax bracket."

"Catherine said you didn't do divorce work."

"I turned him down. But job offers come in clusters, so I won't be in dry dock long. She talked about me?"

"A less assured man might've been jealous."

My drink had gotten warm. I'd been talking too much to pay it any attention. I flagged down our waitress and ordered a Chablis.

"That was Catherine's drink," Prosper said.

"She hated red wine. I can't toast her with cabernet."